New Experience

BOOK THREE

karmen SCOTT

© 2023 Cover Illustration by Noah Quarles of noahalmightyart

Copyright © 2024 Karmen Scott

All rights reserved. No part of this publication may be reproduced, scanned distributed, or transmitted in any manner or by any means, including photocopying, recording, or other electronic or mechanical methods, without the prior written permission of the copyright owner or publisher, except in the case of brief quotations embodied in critical reviews and certain other noncommercial uses permitted by copyright law. Thank you for buying an authorized edition of this book and for complying with copyright laws.

Edited by Brianna Mbog

Reformatted and edited by Karmen Scott (2026)

All chapter art by Noah Quarles of noahalmightyart

ISBN 9798330363032 (Paperback)

Manufactured in the United States

Contents

Disclaimer   1

Dedication   2

Prologue   4

Part One   7

1. Chapter One   8

2. Chapter Two   18

3. Chapter Three   27

4. Chapter Four   34

5. Chapter Five   38

Part Two   46

6. Chapter Six   47

7. Chapter Seven   50

8. Chapter Eight   55

9. Chapter Nine   60

10. Chapter Ten   64

11. Chapter Eleven   69

12. Chapter Twelve   74

13. Chapter Thirteen   79

14. Chapter Fourteen   85

15. Chapter Fifteen   90

16. Chapter Sixteen   96

17. Chapter Seventeen   104

18. Chapter Eighteen   109

19. Chapter Nineteen   116

20. Chapter Twenty   121

Part Three   125

21. Chapter Twenty-One   126

22. Chapter Twenty-Two   134

23. Chapter Twenty-Three   141

24. Chapter Twenty-Four   146

...Don't cry yet...   149

Epilogue I   150

Epilogue II   159

Epilogue III   162

Letter from the Author   167

About Author   169

Sentimental Message   171

Disclaimer

＊ Note to readers: this story contains *"ebonics"*.

According to Google, *ebonics* "is African American English, especially when viewed as a language in its own right rather than as a dialect of standard English."

*Contains some profanity.

*Contains fade-to-black scenes.

*Contains heavy Christian themes.

Dedication

To my sweet baby Angel:

The baby I never got the chance to meet but had the blessing of carrying for a few weeks... A few weeks may not be that big of a deal to most people, but it was everything to me. And losing you hurt more than anything. I may never get to know you or hold you in this lifetime, but I believe that you are running around with Jesus, my baby sisters, and my grandparents, having the time of your life. So, I dedicate this book to you. I love you.

To my babies, Kimberly and Ash:

My babies. I love you guys more than you will ever know. You guys are my living miracles. Kimberly, my first baby and one of my biggest supporters thank you for being my sweet, smart babygirl. I hope I continue to make you proud. To my rainbow baby, Ashley, you are the sweetest little boy, and I am blessed to have you in my life. You came at the perfect time. You are the rainbow that came after the scariest storm I've ever experienced. Thank you, my babies, for loving me and choosing me as your mommy.

To the parents who have lost a little one:

(no matter how far along you were, no matter how much time has passed)

Your experience is valid, and your healing journey is *your* journey. I pray you experience peace and love. I send you all my love and support, and I pray you can feel my hugs from miles away. I love you. God bless you.

Prologue

I t's our wedding day, and I am ecstatic. This felt like a dream. The way the proposal happened still burns in my mind and heart as if it just happened...

June 2018

"Anthony... This is amazing. How did you do this? You know how much I love this place."

He nodded and smiled, "Yeah, that's why I did it. You love to come here, and I wanted to do something special for you just because." I blushed.

"That's very sweet." Soon after, one of the baristas came to our table and sat my regular order on the table in front of me and Anthony's regular order in front of him. We made small talk for a while, but something was off about him. He wasn't as talkative or joking around as he usually does. But I just went along with it because I just figured he had a lot on his mind. We both turned our attention to the singer and live band on the stage. Ironically, she was singing one of my favorite songs, New Balance by Jhene Aiko. I closed my eyes and listened to her sing those beautiful lyrics while humming along with her. This song spoke to me in many ways as it described the way I felt about Anthony.

Then suddenly, I opened my eyes and saw Anthony on the stage where the singer was supposed to be. The band kept playing lowly and Anthony grabbed the mic.

"Kyrah, do you remember when we met in the vending room? I have to tell you that you literally took my breath away from that very moment. After that night, I couldn't get you out of my mind. Every time I left my room, I was hoping that I would see you again so I could at least get your name. Then we bumped into each other, and I knocked all of your food out of your hands," he paused and chuckled. I laughed as tears fell from my eyes.

He continued, "I wish I could say I did that on purpose because I really wanted to know you, but I have to believe that that was God giving me a second chance to make my move. You have changed my life for the better. I will forever be thankful to God for bringing you into my life. I don't think you understand the impact you've had on me. You've made such an impact that I can't even see my life without you in it... And I don't want to..." He stopped, gave the mic back to the singer, and made his way off the stage. He walked towards me, and I could feel my heart about to beat out of my chest. He stood in front of me.

"Kyrah..." he began before he knelt in front of me. More tears spilled from my eyes, and I placed my hand over my mouth. He pulled out a ring box from his pocket and opened it. He looked me deep in my eyes, with tears in his. His deep voice cracked a little.

"Baby girl, I told you I would make this happen one day. This is me keeping my word. I am ready to take the next step with you. I am ready to live the rest of my life with you. Kyrah, will you marry me?"

I nodded so quickly as "yes" fell from my lips. I wrapped my arms around his neck and hugged him tightly. He pulled away and slipped the beautiful diamond ring on my ring finger, then pulled me in for a kiss. Suddenly, I heard cheering and clapping coming from behind me and the lights were turned on. I turned around to find my friends, my family, and his family standing far behind us watching everything unfold...

Tears welled in my eyes as I replayed the day in my mind. I stared at myself in the mirror, taking in my bare face before my bridal makeup was applied. I couldn't believe I was about to marry the man of my dreams and prayers... The one who changed everything... The one who introduced me to new experiences.

"This is it," I said to myself, a smile spreading across my face.

Part One

Chapter One

August 25th, 2019

"Kyrah?" I heard my name through the door followed by a soft knock on the hotel room I was getting ready in. I turned around and saw my mom and dad walking in. My mom instantly covered her mouth when she saw me in my wedding dress with my makeup and hair done. Instead of an all-white dress, I decided to get an off-white A-line dress that fitted around the waist to show off my shape with my back completely out and a long train. I had my hair straightened and styled in a low ponytail that flowed to my mid-back. My makeup was simple and light with a nude lip. I looked at my parents with tears forming.

"You look stunning," my dad said. They walked over to me, and each kissed me on the cheek. I blew out the air that I had been holding in.

Today was the day I was marrying the love of my life, and I was over the moon. Everything leading up to this moment was perfectly aligned. Despite all the obstacles that tried to block us, we overcame them and grew stronger together. I loved this man like no other and I couldn't wait to call him my husband. After talking to my parents for a few minutes, they headed out to make sure everything was ready. After taking a few breaths, I looked at myself in the mirror. I couldn't believe it. I was really about to get married. Just as I was about to cry for the twentieth time today, my big sister, Kyla, Tamra, Raynah, and my best friend, Alana walked up to me. They all beamed at me through the mirror.

"Oh, my gosh," Kyla said as she admired me.

"Kyrah... I am speechless", Alana said.

"Yeah... " Tamra said as she started to tear up. I fanned my eyes and turned around to face them.

"Please don't cry. I'm fighting it myself," I said while laughing a little. Raynah lightly placed her hand on my arm and smiled at me with a tear falling down her cheek.

"You look so beautiful. Are you ready?", she asked. I took a deep breath and smiled.

"Absolutely."

There I stood waiting for my turn to walk down the path to my fiancé. The garden was beautifully decorated just the way we wanted it. Once our song came on, I knew it was time. I took a deep breath trying to calm my anxiety. I didn't have cold feet at all, and I just prayed that he didn't either. My feet started walking towards him as if they had a mind of their own. I stared straight ahead holding my beautiful bouquet of white lilies mixed with white roses. I turned the corner and my eyes landed on him. Our eyes locked and tears welled in my eyes.

He looked down and quickly wiped his eyes. He looked back at me with love.

As I got closer to him, I could feel my heart beating faster. Harder. It felt like it was about to jump out of my chest. It felt as if no one else was there. I couldn't see anyone else but him. We held each other's gaze the entire time. Once my dad gave me away, I handed Kyla, my maid of honor, my bouquet and placed my hands into Anthony's. He looked at me, tears still in his eyes, and smiled.

"You look... breathtaking", he said to me. I smiled.

"So do you..."

Pastor Kendrick guided the rest of the ceremony as we got closer and closer to officially being married. I could barely pay attention to anything else that was going on because my focus was only on Anthony.

"Anthony and Kyrah have written their own vows so now they will exchange them. Anthony will go first." Anthony took a deep breath and looked at the piece of paper that had his vows written on them. He looked at me and smiled as a tear slipped from one of his eyes.

"Kyrah... Wow. I'm tryna focus, but you are blowing my mind right now," he said with a chuckle making everyone laugh. Once everyone stopped laughing, he refocused and cleared his throat.

"Babygirl", he continued, "I am in love with all that you are. I know I bring up how we met in the vending machine room all the time, but it truly is the day that I am most thankful for. That night, I met someone that I didn't know would have such a big impact on my life and on me as a person. It's amazing to see how far we've come. And I want to take the time to thank you for believing in me and allowing me to be in your life... for allowing me to be vulnerable with you. I tell you all the time that you have my heart, and I mean that with everything in me. Thank you for choosing me to be your husband. And I promise...

I vow to ensure that you feel how much I love you every single day for the rest of our lives. I promise you that I am not going anywhere. You stuck wit' me, baby. I love you so much. More than I can put into words. And I pray that every night you will fall asleep knowing that."

By the time Anthony finished his vows, there was not a dry eye in sight. My face was soaked with tears and my heart was warm. His words penetrated my heart. I sighed and gently wiped my tears away.

"Kyrah, you may now say your vows," Pastor Kendrick said.

I giggled. "Well, I'm not sure how I'm gonna compete with that, but I will do my best," I said lightening the mood and making everyone laugh once again. I took a deep breath and started reading the words on the piece of paper in my hands.

"My sweet, charming, handsome, and all-around amazing Anthony... You are the most incredible human I have ever met. I have never felt the way I feel about you for anyone else. It amazes me how someone can walk into your life and just change everything for you...," I paused letting a few tears flow, "and that's exactly what you did." My voice cracked. I felt Anthony give my hands a tight squeeze. I looked up at him and found him smiling at me. "Anthony, I want to thank you for choosing me... for asking me to be your wife. I can't imagine going through the rest of my life without you in it. I would've settled with just being your friend if that meant you got to be in my life. But God had plans for us from day one... This is it. This is what we've both prayed for. God has blessed me... And I am so incredibly thankful. Anthony, I love you. And I can't wait to continue this journey with you."

There really weren't words to explain all that Anthony meant to me, but I did my best to sum it up. I can only pray that during our lifetime together I would be able to show him what he means to me and how much I truly love him. I looked into his eyes and saw our eternity together. It was beautiful. His beautiful brown eyes held my gaze and he smiled. He mouthed "I love you" making my heart melt. *Man, I can't wait to get this man alone.*

"I now pronounce you husband and wife. You may now kiss your beautiful bride," Pastor Kendrick said.

"Finally!" Anthony said, making everyone laugh. He wrapped his arms around my waist and pulled me towards him. His hands rested on the small of my back making my insides twist with excitement. He leaned down and kissed me slowly. We kissed so passionately that I almost forgot we were in a room full of people. He smiled in the kiss before breaking it.

"You better be ready for tonight," he said lowly. I blushed.

"Oh, believe me, I'm ready to get my hands on you," I responded. He pulled away and raised an eyebrow. I giggled and winked in response. We turned towards our guests and held hands. He caressed the back of my hand with his thumb reassuring me. This felt like a dream. I couldn't believe I'd just gotten married.

"I now present to you for the very first time, Mr. and Mrs. Anthony Jamal Wright," Pastor finished just before the music played. Everyone cheered and Anthony and I grinned until our cheeks hurt. We walked down the aisle hand-in-hand ready to have the night of our lives.

***

Anthony and I sat at our reception table and watched everyone dance. Though we'd been celebrating, admittedly I'd been thinking about one thing and that was getting my husband alone. The anticipation for this wedding quickly died down after we said "I do" because I was more than ready to go.

"What you thinkin' about?" Anthony asked. We sat side-by-side holding hands. We both watched as our families and friends enjoyed themselves laughing, dancing, drinking, and just having a good time. I sighed happily.

"I'm just happy," I said finally looking at him. He searched my eyes for something more.

"Me, too," he responded before pausing, "But from the look in your eyes, that's not the only thing you thinkin' about."

I smirked and leaned closer. He bit his bottom lip and looked me up and down.

"And what do you think I'm thinkin' about, Mr. Wright?" I asked rather seductively. He smirked and stroked his beard with his free hand. *My God, he is so fine.*

"I think... you can't stop thinkin' about what I'ma do to you when we leave here... And you might as well forget about our first time in college because that ain't nothin' compared to what I got planned for you... Mrs. Wright," he said in a very low and sexy voice while looking into my eyes. My mouth became a bit dry just from imagining what he could possibly mean. I cleared my throat trying to hold it together. I almost lost my composure, but I had to remember where I was.

"I think it's time to go..." I said as I prepared myself to stand up. He laughed and stopped me.

"Wait, baby. Come dance with me one more time." A puzzled expression spread across my face as I watched him go to the DJ and request a song. I was slightly confused because we'd already had our first dance. Suddenly "New Balance" by Jhene' Aiko blasted through the speakers. I looked at Anthony and blushed at the gesture. We'd decided on "Beautiful Surprise" by India.Arie as our first dance song because that song described us so much when we reconnected. But this song was definitely the song that defined us the most. He walked back over to me and held out his hand for me to grab. I placed my hand in his and we walked towards the dance floor.

Other couples were slow-dancing but made way for us in the middle of the floor. Suddenly everyone else disappeared. It was just us. As I looked into his eyes, I couldn't see or hear anything else but Anthony and Jhene's voice. He leaned down and kissed my forehead before meeting my eyes again.

"You really are the best thing that's ever happened to me. Thank you for still loving me even after everything. You believed in our love despite all odds. You believed enough for both of us when I was struggling to even love myself. I don't know what I would've done without you," I said with tears in my eyes. He exhaled and held me tighter as if he were afraid I'd slip away.

"No, babygirl... *You* are the best thing that ever happened to *me*. I love you way more than you could ever imagine. And I'll never stop loving you. I hope you know that." I smiled and lightly wiped my escaped tears away. He then stopped dancing and all of the surroundings came flooding back. I gave him a confused look and he leaned down to talk in my ear. I felt his hands slide down my back and rest at the top of my butt. His touch made me feel a different type of excitement. I know he could feel the tension radiating off my body. As soon as he opened his mouth to speak, I knew it was time.

"Now, let's go so I can show you...", was the last thing he said before we dismissed ourselves.

Chapter 2

First time...

We walked down the hall to the suite that Anthony booked for us hand-in-hand. We walked quietly, both of us anticipating what was about to happen as soon as we entered that room. He scanned the room key and opened the door for me to walk in first. He grabbed the **Do Not Disturb** sign and I blushed.

"Might as well not even waste time," he said jokingly as he put it on the doorknob and closed the door. I laughed and stared at my husband. He grabbed my hand and led me further into the suite. It was decorated just for us with a large banner that read "Congratulations Newlyweds" and rose petals scattered across the floor. There was a bucket of ice with champagne in the middle of the coffee table along with two champagne glasses. But that's not even what stole my attention. He moved out of the way so I could take in the city scene that was blatantly visible through the large window. He came behind me, wrapped his arms around my waist, and kissed me slowly on the back of my neck. I smiled to myself, leaning my head to the side, giving him more access. He hummed lowly into the crook of my neck, and I closed my eyes in response.

"Anthony, this is beautiful," I said, opening my eyes and taking in the view once again. He turned me around to face him with his arms still around my waist.

"Not as beautiful as you." I blushed and looked down. He let out a chuckle and kissed me on my forehead. The words "come on" escaped his lips and I already knew what that meant. The tone in his voice was significantly different and his voice was deeper. *Oh, he ready—ready...* I thought to myself. I followed Anthony into the master room and my jaw dropped. There were more rose petals and battery-operated candles everywhere. It was beautiful.

"Oh wow... this is real. We're really married," I said more to myself.

He laughed lightly, "Yep. You are officially Mrs. Wright." I smiled and stood in front of him. I leaned in to kiss his lips slowly.

"I love you," I said.

"I love you, too, beautiful." He kissed me again, instantly deepening the kiss. I admittedly was looking forward to this moment. Despite the fact that we'd made mistakes in our past, I was so glad we got to do it right this time. The major difference this time beyond the fact that we are now married is the fact that Anthony is taking his time with me. Nothing is rushed. He slowly unzipped my reception gown, never tearing his lips away from mine. I eagerly gave in and let him do as he pleased. I started to unbutton his shirt and he smirked. I broke the kiss and looked up at him.

"I am so ready to do this," I stated lowly while still holding his shirt open. I looked down and admired his defined abs, instantly blushing.

"Good... I hope you got some rest last night," he responded seductively. My head shot up to meet his gaze. He slowly removed his shirt from his body, never taking his eyes off mine. I was instantly captivated by the expression in his eyes. His lips didn't have to move because his eyes were saying everything. He stared at me with love, gentleness, compassion, and lust. I melted like butter.

After a while, we both stood before one another in our purest forms. We admired one another, something we didn't do in the past. I took this time to take in just how incredibly handsome God created my husband to be. His defined jawline neatly lined up facial hair and hairline, his long locs put up in a bun showing off his handsome face, his full lips, and my favorite part, his chocolate brown eyes. My eyes slowly scanned him, watching him slowly pull his hair out of the bun before shaking his hair. His long locs fell down and flowed down his back. *Good Lord.* I was thankful. And in that moment, all I wanted to do was give him my love.

"You are so beautiful," he said lowly, almost as if he was thinking aloud. Usually, I would feel self-conscious about my body, but the way he was admiring me ignited my confidence.

"Thank you," I said. He gently grabbed my face and kissed me passionately. His strong hands caressed my back and grabbed my butt turning me on even more. A light moan of anticipation escaped my throat just from finally feeling his hands on me. "Touch me, please," I whimpered desperately. One of his hands traveled and explored.

"Right here?" he asked gaining a reaction from me. I gasped and nodded. He smiled into the sensual kiss and allowed his hands to continue to roam all over my body, taking his time to please me. The rest of the night was filled with intense passion and love. Although we'd done it before when we were in college, it was not even close to this night we spent together. We both took our time exploring, carefully and lovingly being gentle with, and overall, selflessly pleasing one another. The moment we'd both been patiently waiting for was finally here and I wanted to take in every second of it.

I woke up the next morning with the sun shining bright on my face. To my surprise, Anthony was not beside me. I sat up and looked around the room trying to see where he'd disappeared.

"Babe?" I waited for a response.

Anthony?" I called out again. Still no response. I furrowed my eyebrows and got out of the bed. Instantly I remembered that I was completely naked. I scrambled into the bathroom and found a robe to throw on before beginning my search to find my husband in this suite. I walked out of the master bedroom and looked around. *No Anthony in sight... where the heck did he go?* I sighed and plopped down on the couch. I then saw a note sitting on the coffee table. I picked it up:

Chapter Two

We walked down the hall to the suite that Anthony booked for us hand-in-hand. We walked quietly, both of us anticipating what was about to happen as soon as we entered that room. He scanned the room key and opened the door for me to walk in first. He grabbed the ***Do Not Disturb*** sign and I blushed.

"Might as well not even waste time," he said jokingly as he put it on the doorknob and closed the door. I laughed and stared at my husband. He grabbed my hand and led me further into the suite. It was decorated just for us with a large banner that read "Congratulations Newlyweds" and rose petals scattered across the floor. There was a bucket of ice with champagne in the middle of the coffee table along with two champagne glasses. But that's not even what stole my attention. He moved out of the way so I could take in the city scene that was blatantly visible through the large window. He came behind me, wrapped his arms around my waist, and kissed me slowly on the back of my neck. I smiled to myself, leaning my head to the side, giving him more access. He hummed lowly into the crook of my neck, and I closed my eyes in response.

"Anthony, this is beautiful," I said, opening my eyes and taking in the view once again. He turned me around to face him with his arms still around my waist.

"Not as beautiful as you." I blushed and looked down. He let out a chuckle and kissed me on my forehead. The words "come on" escaped his lips and I already knew what that meant. The tone in his voice was significantly different and his voice was deeper. *Oh, he ready—ready...* I thought to myself. I followed Anthony into the master room and my jaw dropped. There were more rose petals and battery-operated candles everywhere. It was beautiful.

"Oh wow... this is real. We're really married," I said more to myself.

He laughed lightly, "Yep. You are officially Mrs. Wright." I smiled and stood in front of him. I leaned in to kiss his lips slowly.

"I love you," I said.

"I love you, too, beautiful." He kissed me again, instantly deepening the kiss. I admittedly was looking forward to this moment. Despite the fact that we'd made mistakes in our past, I was so glad we got to do it right this time. The major difference this time beyond the fact that we are now married is the fact that Anthony is taking his time with me. Nothing is rushed. He slowly unzipped my reception gown, never tearing his lips away from mine. I eagerly gave in and let him do as he pleased. I started to unbutton his shirt and he smirked. I broke the kiss and looked up at him.

"I am so ready to do this," I stated lowly while still holding his shirt open. I looked down and admired his defined abs, instantly blushing.

"Good... I hope you got some rest last night," he responded seductively. My head shot up to meet his gaze. He slowly removed his shirt from his body, never taking his eyes off mine. I was instantly captivated by the expression in his eyes. His lips didn't have to move because his eyes were saying everything. He stared at me with love, gentleness, compassion, and lust. I melted like butter.

After a while, we both stood before one another in our purest forms. We admired one another, something we didn't do in the past. I took this time to take in just how incredibly handsome God created my husband to be. His defined jawline neatly lined up facial hair and hairline, his long locs put up in a bun showing off his handsome face, his full lips, and my favorite part, his chocolate brown eyes. My eyes slowly scanned him, watching him slowly pull his hair out of the bun before shaking his hair. His long locs fell down and flowed down his back. *Good Lord*. I was thankful. And in that moment, all I wanted to do was give him my love.

"You are so beautiful," he said lowly, almost as if he was thinking aloud. Usually, I would feel self-conscious about my body, but the way he was admiring me ignited my confidence.

"Thank you," I said. He gently grabbed my face and kissed me passionately. His strong hands caressed my back and grabbed my butt turning me on even more. A light moan of anticipation escaped my throat just from finally feeling his hands on me. "Touch me, please," I whimpered desperately. One of his hands traveled and explored.

"Right here?" he asked gaining a reaction from me. I gasped and nodded. He smiled into the sensual kiss and allowed his hands to continue to roam all over my body, taking his time to please me. The rest of the night was filled with intense passion and love. Although we'd done it before when we were in college, it was not even close to this night we spent together. We both took our time exploring, carefully and lovingly being gentle with, and overall, selflessly pleasing one another. The moment we'd both been patiently waiting for was finally here and I wanted to take in every second of it.

I woke up the next morning with the sun shining bright on my face. To my surprise, Anthony was not beside me. I sat up and looked around the room trying to see where he'd disappeared.

"Babe?" I waited for a response.

Anthony?" I called out again. Still no response. I furrowed my eyebrows and got out of the bed. Instantly I remembered that I was completely naked. I scrambled into the bathroom and found a robe to throw on before beginning my search to find my husband in this suite. I walked out of the master bedroom and looked around. *No Anthony in sight... where the heck did he go*? I sighed and plopped down on the couch. I then saw a note sitting on the coffee table. I picked it up:

> *Good morning, babygirl. I'll be right back. Went to take care of business. I have a surprise for you. Go ahead and order breakfast. I know you hungry ;) I'll see you soon.*
> *I love you.*

I smiled at the note, placed it back on the table, and decided to order some food like he suggested. While looking at the menu, I heard shuffling outside of the main door and the door swung open. Anthony appeared with a surprised look on his face. He smiled as he got closer to me. He leaned down and gave me a quick peck before sitting beside me.

"I take it you just woke up", he said jokingly. I chuckled and nodded.

"Yeah. I just saw your note. I was just about to order some food then get in the shower."

He nodded, then smirked, "I might join you." I stood up to walk towards the master bedroom. I halted and turned around to face him. He stared at me with confusion written across his face.

"You comin'?" I said with a smirk. He hurriedly got off the couch and ran towards me making me laugh. We raced to the bathroom where more love was made.

***

Around 4:00, I was sitting on the bed packing up a few items before Anthony and I were going to leave the hotel we were staying at. We were getting ready to go on our honeymoon and I was overly excited for this trip.

"So, when am I gonna find out where we're going?" I asked Anthony as I stood up and picked up my small carry-on bag. He walked over to me and wrapped his arms around me. He looked down at me with a small smile on his face. He was so perfect, and I couldn't believe he was my husband.

"Well, I think I wanna wait until we get to our gate at the airport," he finally responded.

I playfully rolled my eyes and smacked my teeth.

"Of course, you do. You're the king of surprises." He laughed.

"I am. But I promise you're gonna love it, we're gonna have so much fun." I smiled and bit my bottom lip. He raised his eyebrows and smirked.

"Nah, don't do that. We gotta go. We don't have time for another round," he joked. I rolled my eyes and laughed.

"Well, I guess we'll just have to wait until we get there," I responded. He smiled and kissed me sweetly before removing the bag from my hand.

I was anxious with anticipation as we made our way to the airport. Even though I wanted to ask Anthony where we were going, I decided against it because I knew he wouldn't tell me anyway. We pulled up to the airport and went through the check-in and TSA process. Anthony held my hand the whole time because he knew how anxious airports made me. Everything this man did made me fall deeper for him. My stomach was tied in knots as we approached our gate. He kept my ticket for the most part after I went through TSA. He asked me not to look at it so I wouldn't spoil his surprise. Of course, I complied because I knew he was so excited to surprise me. Suddenly Anthony came to a halt and looked down at me. A cute grin spread across his face.

"Look up," he said as he stepped behind me and wrapped his arms around my waist. I looked at the sign and read the flight destination message. A gasp fell from my lips and my mouth dropped. *St. Lucia*.

"Anthony..." I said as a giggle escaped my lips.

"Surprise," his deep voice rumbled in my ear sending chills down my spine. I turned around and wrapped my arms around his neck. He bent down and kissed my lips so sweetly.

"Thank you, baby," I said. He smiled.

"Anything for you." Our flight wasn't for another two hours so we decided to grab some food and just walk around for a bit. About thirty minutes before boarding, we decided to head back to the gate and wait for them to call flight class.

"One more surprise..." Anthony said. I looked at him puzzled and frowned slightly.

"What you mean?" I asked. He smirked and shrugged.

"Now boarding first class," the voice called over the gate intercom. Anthony stood up and held his hand out for me to grab.

"What are you doing?" I asked. He laughed.

"That's us. Come on." My eyes widened in response. I placed my hand in his and stood up. He handed me my ticket and I read it. First class. I looked at him in awe. He smiled and kissed me on the forehead.

I don't know how he managed to keep all this a secret, but I wasn't complaining. He never ceases to amaze me. After getting our tickets scanned, we walked on the plane hand in hand and sat in our spacious, comfortable seats. I was in heaven.

"Oh, Anthony. I wish this was a private plane," I said as I melted into the seat with my eyes closed. A deep laugh came from his throat.

"A'ight, now. You better watch yourself," he said. I looked at him and smirked.

"You think I'm playin', but I'm dead serious. We're married now. You gon' get it when we get to our destination." He raised an eyebrow and adjusted himself in his seat. I laughed as I watched him struggle to keep himself together.

"You better keep that same energy, too. That's all I'ma say. But I think we better end this conversation right now because we have a four-and-a-half-hour flight ahead of us and that's too long for us to continue this right now," he said lowly. I giggled and snuggled close to him.

"Whatever you say, big daddy," I teased. He sighed.

"Lord God... Help me," he said as he shook his head and laughed.

After a slightly long flight, we landed at our destination and were immediately met with our guide for the trip. He drove us to our resort and showed us some of the sights on the way there. I was barely listening because I was distracted by the beauty that surrounded us. This was new for me, and I couldn't wait to do more things like this with my husband. We pulled into our resort and my mouth dropped. Anthony laughed.

"A whole fly gon' just fly up in there if you don't close your mouth," he joked. I kissed my teeth and rolled my eyes.

"Shut up," I responded laughing. The guide opened our door, and we climbed out of the car. While we waited for him to get our bags from the trunk, Anthony wrapped his arms around me from behind and leaned in my ear to speak.

"What you think?" he asked. I smiled and exhaled.

"It's beautiful. Thank you so much." He turned me around to face him.

"This is nothing. Plenty more of this to come for the rest of our lives... As long as I get to see that beautiful smile on your face." I blushed as I looked into his eyes. He leaned down and kissed me so sweetly. Before I knew it, I was getting lost in the kiss until our guide interrupted us.

"Mr. and Mrs. Wright [*I'll never get used to that...*], your bags are ready, and I want to say thank you for visiting St. Lucia. Please enjoy your stay!" he said enthusiastically. A friendly smile spread across my face in response.

"Thank you, sir," Anthony said with his arms still wrapped around me. He unwrapped his arms and grabbed our bags.

"Come on," he said, signaling me to walk ahead of him. We walked into the building, and I looked around, taking in my surroundings as Anthony got our room keys and everything set up for us. After a few minutes, we headed to our suite. As soon as we walked into the room, I couldn't believe my eyes. It was absolutely breathtaking. There was a beautiful entranceway into the kitchen and dining area with a gorgeous living room area topped off with a nice balcony over the beach. Then the bedroom was beyond description as well as the bathroom. I sighed in marital bliss. Anthony led me to the couch, and we sat for a minute.

"This is... amazing," I said leaning my head back on the couch.

He smiled, "I'm glad you like it. We have so much to do on this resort, so we won't be bored."

I nodded, "I'm looking forward to it." He eyed, me making me give him a puzzled expression in response.

"What?" I asked with a smirk.

He smirked back. "There's something else we gotta do first, though."

"Oh yeah? And what's that?" He stood up and held out his hand. I grabbed it and stood up as I looked up at him. He then picked me up bridal style making me squeal and laugh.

"I gotta see if you gon back up all that mouth you had on the plane," he responded. I rolled my eyes and laughed.

"Don't roll them eyes. We finna go christen this room," he said as he started walking towards the bedroom.

"Oh, God," I said in laughter.

"Yeah, that's exactly who you finna be callin' for."

Chapter Three

HONEYMOON BLISS...

The next few days were perfect. Anthony and I spent so much time relaxing, exploring the island, and of course, exploring each other. It was better than I ever could have imagined. After borderline stressing about the wedding planning, this was just what I needed: alone time with my husband. I felt like I was on top of the world, and nothing could bring me down.

It's our last night on our honeymoon before we head back home and start our lives together. We were both getting ready for our final dinner which was put together by the resort. We were flirting and checking each other out.

"Who you tryna look good for?" he asked jokingly while brushing his beard in the mirror. I met his eyes and smirked.

"Who else would I look this good for?" I asked shyly. He bit his bottom lip and put his beard brush down. He stood behind me and wrapped his arms around my waist. He placed kisses on my neck making me giggle.

"Anthony, stop," I laughed. He hummed and buried his face deeper in my neck.

"You smell good," he complimented. My face burned with blush from all the love and affection I was receiving.

Before I could respond, Anthony's phone rang. He checked the caller ID and instantly his smile turned into a slight frown.

"It's my supervisor," he said.

I frowned, "I thought he knew we were on our honeymoon."

He shrugged, "I thought so, too," he started. He looked at me with the sincerest expression. "Do you mind if I answer this?" I smiled in return as my heart warmed after that sincere question. I loved that he considered my feelings even though I didn't even think twice about it.

"Of course not, babe." He smiled and gave me a quick kiss. He walked away and answered the call.

"Hello?" he said as he walked out on the balcony. While he was on the phone, I proceeded to get ready for our dinner date at one of the resort restaurants. As I was applying my mascara, I noticed Anthony came in with a defeated expression. I immediately stopped and turned to face him.

"What's wrong, babe?" He sighed as he walked closer to me.

"Well... What you wanna hear first? The good or the not-so-good?" he asked as he sat in one of the chairs in the bathroom corner. I chuckled.

"Well... start with the good, first, I guess." I sat in the chair across from him. He grabbed my hands and gently held them.

"Okay... Well, I'm up for a promotion. I'll be overseeing the trainees for the HR department during training and stuff. I'll also be a team leader to help guide them during the job." I smiled widely.

"Babe, that's awesome! Congratulations!" I pulled him in for a hug. He hugged me back, but I could tell he was dreading telling me the next part. And part of me had an inkling that it would be something that would majorly affect our marriage.

"Thanks, baby... But we'll have to move," he said while still holding me. I slowly removed myself from his embrace and looked at him with a slight frown. I chuckled.

"Move? Like to another city?" He twisted his lips, trying to find the words to say.

"I wish... We'd have to move to Seattle." I felt as if all the oxygen had left my body as I just sat there and stared at him. I wasn't sure if I was hearing him correctly.

"H-huh?" I asked in disbelief. He exhaled and looked down for a second before meeting my eyes again.

"They're building a new site and put my name in the pool for the HR department when they open next year..." he drifted off. The silence grew for a moment while we were both in deep thought.

"Baby, listen," he said, breaking the silence, "Let's not think about that right now. This is our last night before we go back home. So, tonight, I wanna enjoy this time stress-free, spending time with you, enjoying dinner with you, and making love to you." I blushed at the last statement. He held my hands and kissed them.

"You wanna do what to me?" I asked with a smirk. He raised an eyebrow.

"A'ight now... Don't start somethin' you can't finish."

I laughed and pulled him in for a hug. He wrapped his strong arms around my waist allowing me to melt in his embrace.

"I love you," I said.

"And I love you."

We enjoyed the rest of the evening just like we planned to. The dinner the resort planned for us was absolutely beautiful. We had champagne, a seafood medley, and a delicious dessert to share. Once we got back to our room, Anthony wasted no time keeping his word. He took his time with me and made me feel like the most loved person in the world. He was so attentive to me and my body's needs. I couldn't even begin to imagine anyone else being able to please me like he does. We ended the night in each other's arms, and I was so happy to wake up in his arms the next morning.

***

The sun shined through the window waking me out of my sleep. I sat up and turned to look at Anthony who was snoring. I laughed and got out of the bed. I grabbed my robe and stepped outside on the balcony to take in the beach scenery one last time.

"Thank you, God, for this... You have truly been good to me..." Tears welled in my eyes from gratitude. "I have come a long way from where I was in college. I never thought I'd be here, married, on a honeymoon with the love of my life... You brought me out of that deep depression that I thought I'd always be stuck in. You helped me graduate from college and now I'll be starting a new journey in furthering my college career..." My voice cracked and I choked up. "Anyway... I just wanna say thank you... For everything..."

I felt strong arms wrap around me, and I relaxed into the embrace. None of this felt real. I remember praying for this when I was younger.

"Hey, beautiful," he said lowly. I exhaled and smiled. I turned around to face him and look at his handsome face.

"Hey, husband." He planted a kiss on my forehead before studying my face. Concern spread across his face which convinced me that he saw my tear-stained cheeks.

"You cryin'?" he asked. I chuckled.

"Yeah... But I'm okay. They were tears of gratitude, don't worry your handsome self."

He chuckled and kissed me on the forehead again.

"Just makin' sure. You look so beautiful right now, though."

I blushed, "Stop lying." He shook his head. His eyebrows furrowed and pulled me closer to him. My heart was beating outside of my chest as I looked into his eyes.

"I'd never lie about your beauty... You are literally the most beautiful woman I've ever laid eyes on. And I'll never get tired of telling you that... Or showing you that for that matter..." He bit his bottom lip and leaned down to kiss me.

"Anthony..." I responded, sighing into the kiss.

"I know we have to go soon... But I think we have time for one more round," he said breaking the kiss. I removed myself from his embrace and walked back towards the balcony door.

"I think so, too," I responded.

"Girl, get in that room," he said as he walked towards me. I squealed when he started chasing me to bed.

On the flight back home, my mind was filled with the happy memories I'd just made with my husband. This trip was one I'd never forget and made me look forward to all the things we'd do in our lifetime together. However, I couldn't help but think about the call he'd received from his supervisor about his new position. Would we really have to relocate? My stomach knotted as I thought about the distance between our home and Seattle, Washington.

The last thing I wanted was for Anthony to think that I didn't support him and didn't want to follow him wherever he had to go. I just wish it didn't have to be so soon.

I shook those thoughts out of my head as we landed. We made our way off the plane and waited for our luggage.

"Did you have fun?" he asked me while holding my hand. I smiled and nodded.

"I did. Thank you for secretly planning such an amazing trip."

He kissed me on the forehead, "More to come." We finally found our luggage on the conveyor belt and quickly grabbed it so we could head home. Thankfully our ride was outside waiting for us so we wouldn't have to wait. I couldn't wait to get home. I enjoyed the trip, but I was looking forward to sleeping in my own bed underneath my own blankets.

After another two and a half hours of traveling on the road from Atlanta to Augusta, my brother, Kyrie dropped us off at our apartment on his way to his apartment.

"Thanks, Ky," I said as he helped Anthony bring our bags into our apartment.

"No problem. I just hope y'all brought me back somethin'," he joked. I rolled my eyes.

"Yeah, some stories and memories," I responded. He smacked his teeth.

"Y'all suck," he said.

Anthony laughed, "We'll bring the souvenirs to the parents' house on Sunday."

"See, that's why I like you. My sister on the other hand—"

"Boy, get out," I interrupted him. It was always like this with us, but he was one of my best friends. With us being so close in age, it sometimes felt like we were twins. But more than anything, I loved the relationship he and Anthony had developed.

After they finished bringing in our stuff, Kyrie headed out leaving us alone in our new place. I looked around feeling mixed emotions knowing that there was a possibility we wouldn't be staying here much longer. I walked into our bedroom and sat on my side of the bed to take my shoes off. Anthony soon followed behind and plopped down beside me lying on his back.

"You good?" he asked with his tired voice. I smirked.

"Yeah, just ready to get some sleep."

"Let me put you to sleep," he said. I looked at him and noticed his eyes were already closed.

"Boy, you already falling asleep," I responded with a laugh. He laughed sleepily as I laid beside him and cuddled in his arms, slowly drifting off the sleep.

Chapter Four

THE REAL BEGINNING...

Two Months Later

Our lives together post-honeymoon seemed to be picking up quickly. We moved into our small but quaint 2-bedroom apartment in Augusta, GA, and adjusted with little-to-no issues. Married life, so far, has been a fairytale. Anthony has been such an attentive and amazing husband. It's like he went from being an amazing boyfriend to an even better husband, which I didn't even think was possible. We spent most of our nights talking and cuddling. We mostly talked about our plans for our future family. Starting a family with Anthony was something I couldn't wait to do. I looked forward to the day I carried his children.

Our daily routine consisted of us both waking up early in the morning after Anthony's alarm rang. He gets up and gets himself ready while I make us both coffee along with a nice breakfast. We eat breakfast at our table and flirt a little. I truly enjoyed our life together so far. While Anthony was off at work, most days I'd usually be busy with school since I started a master's program to continue my writing degree. Other days I would just busy myself with home projects or go hang out with one of my family members.

I stared at Anthony as I sat across from him at our small dining table while he was working on a work-related project and I was sipping a cup of coffee, working on some schoolwork. He glanced at me and smirked.

"You know, they say it's impolite to stare," he joked. I playfully rolled my eyes.

"You would know, wouldn't you? May I recall you staring at me when we first met in the vending machine room?" He looked up and smacked his lips.

"Nah. That's different. That booty was lookin' too nice. I couldn't help it." My jaw dropped as he burst into a fit of laughter. I soon joined him. Once we calmed down, I sighed.

"What's on your mind, baby girl?" he asked sincerely. I sighed.

"I was thinking about this move..."

He looked at me sincerely, "You scared?" I shrugged.

"A little. I don't know... I thought we were gonna settle down here in Augusta. Washington is so... far," I chuckled a little. He smiled.

"I know... I didn't think I'd get that promotion, to be honest. I wasn't anticipating them asking us to pick up and move either... But I don't think I have any other options, baby."

I sighed, "That's true..." I drifted off. My mind started racing about the different possibilities that awaited us in Seattle. Our love has stood strong through a lot, but would this move change that? Would it draw us closer, or would it split us apart? I wasn't ready for this change.

"Babygirl, I can see your mind spiraling," Anthony said, interrupting my thoughts. "Listen, it's okay. This is just a new beginning for us, alright?" I smiled a little, still feeling the anxiety fill up my stomach.

"Yep... New beginning..." I finally responded, every word dripping with uncertainty.

"Girl, you what?" my best friend, Alana, asked me. We were at our favorite frozen yogurt spot that we'd been coming to since we were in high school. I put a spoonful of the froyo in my mouth and nodded in defeat.

"Yes. We have to move to Seattle, and I have not told my family, yet. I am freaking out, but I'm not sure what exactly it is that I'm freaking out about."

She sighed, "Okay, time to unpack."

I chuckled, "Alana, what? —"

She shook her head interrupting me.

"We gotta figure out what it is that's holding you back. I've known you long enough to know that you are self-sabotaging and something's keeping you from wanting to move far away with your husband. I could understand if you were going by yourself, but you're literally going away with the man of your dreams. So, Kyrah... What's going on? What are you afraid of?"

I sat and thought about what she'd said. I mean, she wasn't lying, but I honestly couldn't pinpoint exactly what it was that I was afraid of. Was it the sudden change? The distance? Or just afraid of not being able to connect with other people? All of the above? I just couldn't figure it out. And the last thing I wanted was to move to a whole new state and not be able to meet and befriend other people. I struggled with that enough in college. I didn't want to do it again.

"Alana, I wish I could tell you, honestly. It's just... How could this happen so suddenly? We just settled into our cute little apartment, and we're comfortable here. I'm comfortable. But I don't know how to tell him that without hurting him. That's the last thing I want to do."

"Have you guys talked about this yet? How you're feeling, I mean."

I nodded and exhaled sharply.

"We have... and we both kind of just brushed it off. I played it off like it wasn't a big deal instead of just being completely honest with him. He just seems so excited... I don't want to ruin that for him. Lana, he's worked so hard for this position, and I don't want to be the one to stand in the way of his achievement."

Empathy spread across her face as she listened. Alana had witnessed my life journey since we were 15 and she knew better than anybody that I always dreaded sudden change. I like living comfortably and having to move all the way to Seattle was far from that.

"Kyrah, at the end of the day, he's your husband. I know that something is scaring you, but don't let that stop you from being supportive of him."

I sat there for a moment contemplating on her words before nodding while stirring my froyo.

"Yeah..." I finally responded. *I just need to talk to him...*

Chapter Five

Our apartment was cool, but the tension was thick and heated. I took a chance and tried talking to Anthony about how I was feeling, except I was emotional and so was Anthony in his own way. We hadn't argued like this since college, only this time, neither of us could walk away. I wanted to run and hide, but I knew I couldn't do that. Both of us tried our best to make points and get the other to understand, but our emotions were so high that we were too busy listening to respond... Or maybe it was just me that was overly emotional.

"Anthony, you're not listening to what I'm saying. I'm trying to tell you that I'm just nervous about moving." I searched his eyes for some type of emotion. All I could see was confusion.

"I get that, but we're a family now. And we talked about this already—"

"I know that. I was there," I responded sharply. I was now responding emotionally. He frowned.

"Ay, what's with the attitude? I'm just tryna talk to you."

I sighed, "Well, I'm trying to express my feelings, but it seems like it's going in one ear and out the other…" I retorted lowly. He shook his head.

"You not the only one with feelings, bro…" I rolled my eyes, blinking the tears away.

"Yeah, I know that… but you're dismissing mine—"

"No, you're dismissing mine! I'm telling you that I understand you're nervous but it hurts me to hear you say that you care more about staying here with your side of the family instead of relocating with me so we can start our own family. What about me, Kyrah? How would you feel if I said I didn't wanna move away from my family and stayed in Atlanta instead of coming here to Augusta?"

Tears welled in my eyes as I listened to his words. He was right, but the stubbornness in me wouldn't budge no matter how hard I tried to fight it.

"That's not fair…" my voice cracked as tears streamed down my face.

"It's not? That's funny because I don't think it's fair that I gotta share my wife with other people. I don't think it's fair that my wife would rather put other people's feelings over mine…" he paused, "but I guess that's just it." By the time he finished talking, my chest felt heavy. I didn't know how to respond.

"What's just it?" I asked fearful of what he would say next. He stood up and sighed. *Oh no. He's gonna leave me…*

"We both have different priorities, I guess… I need some air." He shook his head and walked out of our room. I sat in disbelief. Suddenly a soft sob escaped my chest and tears poured from my eyes. A simple conversation turned into a disagreement in a matter of seconds. I hated it when we weren't on the same page. It left me heartbroken. I tried to think of ways to get him to come back so we could reconcile but I came up with nothing. I just wanted him to understand where I was coming from. The last thing I wanted to do was hurt him. I've always hated to see sadness in Anthony's eyes. His beautiful brown eyes always had such life in them; a brightness that couldn't be duplicated. All he had to do was look at me and I could instantly feel my day brighten. But when the brightness was dimmed and replaced with hurt, anger, betrayal, sadness, or any other dark emotion, it broke my heart... and I just wanted to fix it. It hurts worse when I know I'm the reason for it.

I cried for what felt like hours. I did my best to calm myself down, but every time I thought about Anthony, I cried harder.

"God... I messed up... what am I supposed to do...?" I prayed in between tears. Feeling hopeless, I lay down.

After lying there for a few minutes, Anthony walked in. He looked at me. I noticed he had on some slides, and he had the car keys. I sat up in fear as my mind started thinking the worst. He leaned against the doorframe and stared at me.

"Put some shoes on," he said before walking away. I quickly got out of the bed, grabbed my phone, put some slides and a hoodie on, and followed him out of the room. We walked out of the apartment in silence. He opened the car door for me, and I got in. He got on the driver's side, started the car, and we drove off in silence. Memories of when he took me on a car drive in college during my season of deep depression flooded my brain. That was the night I realized I still loved him. I looked out the window and chewed on my bottom lip to stop myself from feeling anxious from the deafening silence. Interrupting my thoughts, Anthony exhaled.

"Babygirl... listen," he started, "I'm sorry for getting emotional. I understand your feelings completely. Trust me, I do. Starting over in a new place is scary." I looked at him and listened carefully. He glanced at me before looking back at the road.

"I'm scared, too," he continued. My heart dropped after hearing his words. I hadn't considered that he was afraid, too. I only thought about myself. "But, if you're with me, it'll be worth it... and we can start over together... you and me... but we can't work this out if you're not willing to at least try with me." A deep sigh fell from my lips. I chose my words carefully. He reached out and caressed my thigh. I placed my hand on top of his, taking in the intimate moment.

"You have nothing to apologize for... You're right... I'm sorry for not considering your feelings in all this. That wasn't fair." He nodded and I exhaled softly. A light chuckle left my lips. "I just knew you were about to leave me...," I finally responded. He grabbed a hold of my hand and lightly squeezed it.

He glanced over at me and frowned, "Nah, never that, baby... It's just a disagreement. We're good... We gon be straight, babygirl. I promise." I smiled and exhaled.

When we got back home, we discussed the move more, but this time, I was more understanding of his side. Every day I got to see a more vulnerable side of him that made me understand him a lot more. If he hadn't told me that he was scared about the move, I wouldn't have considered that because he appeared to be so sure about it. But in reality, he was feeling the same hesitance I was, and I was too blinded by my own selfishness to see that.

***

The Next Day

"Mama, what time will dinner be ready?" I asked my mom over Face-Time. I was pulling my hair up in a puff about to get dressed so we could go to my parents' house for Sunday dinner.

"Should be ready in an hour. What time y'all coming?" she asked while stirring a pot of mashed potatoes.

"Probably leaving in like the next 30 minutes or so."

"Okay, well, we'll see y'all in a little bit."

"Okay, see you." I ended the call and put the finishing touches on my hair. Anthony walked in and eyed me with a smirk. He came behind me and wrapped his arms around my waist. He slowly tried to untie my robe and I stopped him by lightly smacking his hand.

"Can I help you?", I asked giggling.

"You could if we ain't have to go to your parents' house." I rolled my eyes and removed his arms from around me.

"Anthony. Cut it out." He laughed and walked towards the mirror to fix his hair into a low bun. I walked into the room and took my robe off to change into my outfit. I put on a pair of high-waisted jeans and a black crop top. I paired it with a pair of black and white high-top vans and a black cardigan. I put my glasses on and walked back into the bathroom to make sure I looked okay. Anthony looked at me with a genuine expression.

"You look beautiful," he said as if he could read my mind. I smiled.

"Thank you..."

"You ready to tell them about the move?" He asked. Admittedly, I'd been keeping it a secret because I wasn't ready to face the reality of not being able to see my family often. The thought of leaving everything and everyone I know behind was too depressing. I sighed and shook my head "No".

"Not really... but I guess we have to, huh?" He put his beard brush down and turned to face me. He grabbed one of my hands and pulled me closer to him. Wrapping his arms around my waist, he kissed my forehead lightly.

"I'll be right there with you." While I appreciated the gesture and his words, they didn't exactly bring me the comfort I needed. Perhaps it was because I was worried that this move could greatly affect our marriage… Maybe I was afraid that if our marriage fell apart, the move would've been for nothing. I closed my eyes to try and slow my brain down but failed miserably. Like clockwork, Anthony pulled me out of it.

"Whatever your brain is telling you right now, don't worry about it, okay?" He said gently. I exhaled as I looked into his eyes.

"Okay" fell from my lips without hesitation.

"Now, let's go eat," he said before giving me another quick peck on the forehead.

After grabbing our belongings, we made our way out of the house and headed to my parents' house. The whole ride I couldn't stop overthinking this conversation. I wasn't worried about their reaction, per se. I was just scared… scared of change.

We arrived at my folks' place after a 25-minute drive. Anthony parked the car and rushed out of the car over to my side to open my door. We walked hand in hand to the front door making small talk. I rang the doorbell and a few seconds later, my mom opened the door.

"Hey, babies!" She gave us both a hug and we all walked to the family room. I was greeted by my dad and my siblings. I did my best to get out of my head but for some reason, I was overthinking the whole thing. *I'm grown! And I'm married! Why am I so nervous?*

We all conversed for a while; however, my mind was elsewhere. I'm not sure where the uncertainty of this move was coming from exactly, but maybe I could talk to my mom for some advice after we told them the news.

Everyone chatted as we all sat around the living room eating our dinner. I watched Anthony interact with my family and it warmed my heart. There was nothing this man could do that would make me not love him. I took a sip of my Cola and looked down at my plate.

"So, y'all said y'all had some news for us?" My dad said cutting straight to the chase. Typical.

"Yeah!" Anthony started, "I got a promotion at my job. I'll be overseeing the trainees for HR."

"Wow! That's awesome, man. Congratulations," my dad said.

"Thank you!" And then it got quiet. A quiet sigh escaped my chest as I felt the anxiety building up.

"I'll take a wild guess that there's a catch to this," Kyrie said before sipping his drink. I raised an eyebrow as I noticed he looked at me while saying it.

"Yeah... we have to move to Seattle," Anthony finished. Everyone's eyes grew big before they all... smiled? *What the heck?*

"Wait, why are y'all smiling?" I asked confused.

My older brother, Kyle, laughed. "You want us to be angry?"

I chuckled, "No, I guess not." I stole a quick glance at Anthony who was looking at me with a loving gaze. I smiled and looked back at my family. "I guess I was nervous because we're all so close and I wasn't sure how you would feel about me having to move so far away."

"Kyrah, you're married now. Anthony is your family. He's your priority, right?" my dad asked me. He was right. Anthony is my priority, now, and that's all that should matter. Memories of our heated argument flooded my memory and I had to fight the tears that threatened to fall. He was right. I was putting my family's feelings over his and that hurt him. I understand it clearly now. There was only one thing to do... and that was to follow him wherever he needed to go and to trust him.

I nodded my head. "Yeah, he is," I answered while looking at him. He smiled warmly.

"Alright, then. Don't worry about us. We'll be fine," my dad finished.

"Plus, I'll have somewhere to visit," my mom chimed in. I laughed and sipped the rest of my Cola.

We stayed with my family a little while longer before deciding to head out and spend the rest of our evening together. Anthony and I barely made it into the house without ripping each other's clothes off. I guess the little breakthrough moment at my parents' house really got to him and I was glad it did. Needless to say, we spent the rest of the night expressing the love and solidifying the bond we'd been building over the years. I loved this man with everything in me and I wanted to make sure he knew that.

He planted soft kisses on my neck as he held me close, making me sigh in pleasure and satisfaction as a response. He loved me better than anybody else ever could. Every time we made love, it was more and more obvious that we were made for each other. And it also proved that I wanted to follow him no matter where we landed.

Part Two

Chapter Six

DECISIONS (ANTHONY'S THOUGHTS)

Ten Months Later

Making the decision to move to a completely different state far away from everything we knew was a tough one, especially now that a pandemic had hit the world full force without warning. There were so many protocols we needed to go through before being able to make this move and at one point, I was starting to think we wouldn't be able to go at all.

On top of all that, constantly going back and forth with Kyrah about this move in the beginning was draining me, and I was starting to wonder if it was worth it. I needed her more than I needed this job. Although it was scary for both of us, it was a great opportunity for me and my career. But sometimes I couldn't help but often wonder if I was being selfish in all of this. So, when she finally realized that she could always depend on me no matter where we ended up, it warmed my heart and opened my eyes to see that I couldn't do this without her. In the end, I was thankful that everything worked out so we could start this new journey together.

I watched her as she carefully wrapped our coffee mugs in old newspapers before placing them into a box. We were spending our one-year anniversary weekend getting some packing done before the movers came to pick our things up. This move was a big one and I could feel the excitement in my body for this new adventure with the person I love the most.

"Okay, that's the last mug," she said after carefully placing it into the box. That beautiful smile spread across her beautiful face. I walked over to the couch and motioned for her to come over with me.

"Come take a break," I said. She walked over to me and made herself comfortable on my lap. It was silent for a moment as we both just sat in each other's presence. She snuggled closely to me as my arms tightened around her. I'm sure she was in deep thought. I wasn't naïve to the fact that she was still scared. Hell, so was I. But I appreciated her taking this leap with me.

"Baby...," she started. Her eyes met mine as she lifted her head off my chest. I raised an eyebrow waiting for her to continue.

"I just want you to know that despite the earlier conversations we had about this move, I'm ready to do this with you. One of the things I've learned in this short amount of time we've been married is..." she paused for a second searching my eyes with so much love in hers. "I can go anywhere with you as long as I'm with you. I can face anything as long as I'm with you."

There was nothing that could wipe the smile off my face. No other words were needed. My lips were immediately drawn to hers. Those words ignited something in me that deepened my love in that moment. She shifted her body and straddled her legs on either side of my hips.

Soft sighs left her lips as my hands roamed up and down her back. I couldn't wait any longer and it was clear that she needed exactly what I needed in that moment. I picked her up and carried her to our bed for one last time in this apartment... our first home. Our sex life was very healthy so far and I hoped it stayed that way.

I wasted no time taking her clothes off, exploring her like only I knew how to. Her response to my touch always pleased me in an unexplainable way. She squirmed, squealed, and whimpered as I made love to her. Groans filled my throat from hearing her and feeling her. Every time with her was magical and this was no different. Our bodies were made for each other. It wasn't as evident when we first did it in college, but after we waited until our wedding night, it became clear. It made it worth the wait. And now we get to do this all this time, expressing our love for one another when words just failed us. We marked our territory in this apartment and now that it was time to move on, this seemed to be the best way to say goodbye. I wanted to salvage this moment with her... just this one moment... because in the next few days, everything was going to change.

Chapter Seven

MOVING ON...

"A'ight man, just sign here and we'll get this stuff shipped out to your new place. Should be there within the next week or so," one of the movers said to Anthony. He signed the electronic document and handed it back to the mover. I watched as all the movers picked up our belongings, walked out of the door, and disappeared outside.

Surprisingly a sense of calm settled into my heart that overrode the fear I once felt. I sighed as I walked towards Anthony who wore a small smile on his face. He wrapped his arms around my waist before kissing me softly on the forehead.

"You alright?" he asked. I nodded while chewing my bottom lip.

"Yeah... Just can't believe how fast this day got here."

"I know," he exhaled. "We're gonna make the best of it."

I looked up at him and smiled. Standing on my tippy toes, I leaned forward to kiss him on the cheek, and he smiled in response.

"Alright guys… I guess this is it," I said to my family with tears in my eyes. They all came to see us off at the airport shuttle office. My eyes shifted between everyone's faces, taking in the sad expressions in their eyes. I know they were happy and excited for us, but it didn't make this moment any easier.

"We'll come visit you guys soon. Just let us know when you guys get settled," my dad said with a slight crack in his voice. I nodded as I wiped the tears from my cheeks. He embraced me and kissed my hair.

"Be safe," he said lowly. A soft sob filled and escaped my chest involuntarily. Before I knew it, my whole family was embracing me and Anthony in hugs, making this whole departure emotional. The only words that were spoken were "I love you" with tears. I smiled at everyone and took hold of Anthony's hand. He lightly squeezed my hand, reassuring me that he was with me the whole time.

I looked out the window of the shuttle not even noticing the other passengers boarding on. My family waved, wiping their eyes with sad smiles. I waved back with blurred vision. My eyes closed as I felt Anthony wrap his arm around me pulling me towards him for comfort. The driver started the van and we drove off, watching my family disappear in the distance. The whole ride to the airport was a blur. My phone couldn't distract me no matter how hard I tried. The only thing I could find comfort in was feeling Anthony's breathing as I cuddled on his chest. He softly caressed my hip to comfort me. It felt as if he was trying to remind me that we were in this together. And I held on to that one small, yet important reminder.

After arriving at the airport, Anthony did everything he could to lift my spirits and it truly helped. I couldn't help but admire how attentive he is to me. He shows me how he cares and pays attention to even the slightest detail in me. Yes, I was feeling sad, but I couldn't fight the joy I was feeling to be going on this journey with him. I kept telling myself that I was going on a fun adventure with my best friend. Truthfully, it was starting to feel that way. He was so tender and loving the whole way there. He found one of my favorite movies on the airplane and we watched it as my head rested on his shoulder. Periodically, he would check on me by glancing down at me and leaving soft kisses on my head. But once we landed, everything became real. Everything was different. And the unfamiliarity triggered a little anxiety.

I looked around the Seattle-Tacoma International Airport feeling lost. I felt like a foreigner. My breathing was ragged with anxiety in my belly. *Slow deep breaths. Inhale. Exhale.* I could hear Moriah's voice from the sessions I went to before moving. Nothing was relieving this feeling. I closed my eyes hearing the busyness even at nighttime. I was unsure if it was the move itself or just the number of people around me that was making me feel this way. Anthony's calming presence surrounded me as he gently pulled me into his strong arms.

"Hey, I'm right here." My eyes opened and met his. He smiled warmly. "Let's get our bags and head out. Our car is here." I nodded and followed him to baggage claim then outside to the Lyft.

The ride to our new home was quiet... at least to me, it was. Somehow, I managed to zone out Anthony and the driver's light conversation. My brain was as busy as the airport.

Anthony has his career and his life figured out. But what am I going to do? While being a stay-at-home wife sounds good, is that something I really want to do? Should I get a job? Well... Anthony makes more than enough for us to live from. And he's made sure our savings are stocked. Maybe a hobby? But what about when we start having children? I'm pretty sure we'll start trying soon... Maybe I can—

"Babygirl, we're here," Anthony said lowly grabbing my attention. *I really need to stop overthinking this... We're going to be fine. I'm going to be fine.*

I walked slowly behind Anthony into our new red brick town-house. It was cute... Who am I kidding; it was gorgeous. Definitely an upgrade from where we come from. Thankfully, Anthony's job was paying for us to stay here, otherwise, we'd be in a smaller apartment than before. Anthony made a lot of money, but Seattle is expensive. I was thankful for the accommodation in exchange for us having to uproot our lives and move across the country. It's the least they could do, right?

The inside of the house was just as beautiful, if not more. It was modern. The kitchen contained espresso-colored cabinets, a steel refrigerator, a black and steel-colored combo stove with a black, gray, and dark stone layered brick wall behind it, a large island with a stoned-colored countertop and a deep steel sink, and a steel dishwasher.

It was stunning. The living room was spacious. In an instant, my brain birthed numerous ideas for décor and ways to make this place feel like home, not just for me but for Anthony, too. A smile invaded my lips as I looked around.

Anthony walked back into the house with the last of the bags we were able to bring with us.

"Anthony, this is beautiful."

He chuckled, "I know right? The pictures didn't do it any justice."

I just couldn't wait to get our stuff in here. I was just glad we ordered our new bedroom set to be delivered tomorrow; otherwise, it would be a long, painful week on an air mattress, that's for sure. After placing the last bag down, Anthony walked over to me and hugged me from behind. I exhaled in his embrace, allowing my body to relax in his comfort.

"Thank you for doing this with me. I know it's been scary, but I promise I'll make it worth your while," he reassured me. A giggle fell from my lips as I turned around to face him wrapping my arms around his torso.

"I know one way you can make it worth my while," I teased with a small smirk.

H bit his lip and chuckled, "You so nasty."

I rolled my eyes, "Whatever, you like it."

"I do. Let's go do that, now." A yelp escaped my lips as he swiftly threw me over his shoulders and carried me upstairs.

Chapter Eight

Beautiful Surprise

Adjusting was a lot easier than I'd expected. Thankfully, Raynah and her now husband, Tommy, Tamra, and Sean (who are now engaged) offered to come spend a week in Seattle to help us settle in. I couldn't contain my excitement to see my friends again. Since the pandemic started, I didn't think I would be able to see them for another year, but thankfully, everything was slowly but surely returning back to normal. Plus, I'm even more excited now that Anthony has developed a close relationship with Tommy and Sean.

Anthony walked into the guest bedroom and hugged me from behind as I was putting a pillowcase on one of the pillows for the guest bed. I smirked to myself and deeply inhaled his scent. *Girl, not right now. Control yourself.*

"Hey," he said deeply into my neck.

"Hey, yourself." He left small kisses on my neck before removing his embrace.

"Have they landed yet?" he asked me before grabbing a pillowcase and lending me a hand. I nodded.

"Yep. They're headed this way now."

He smiled, "You excited?"

I paused and smiled widely. "I am. I haven't seen them in a minute."

He chuckled, "I know. Y'all will be in your own world not paying any of us menfolk any attention."

I winked, "As long as you know." It was silent for a moment and I giggled to myself.

"You know, Tam thinks I'm pregnant," I blurted out. Anthony stopped and glanced at me with a raised brow. I studied his face and noticed him fighting back a smile.

"Are you?" he asked skeptically.

"I'on know... The way we have sex, I wouldn't be surprised." A rumble of laughter interrupted the short silence that fell over the room after my response. I laughed and placed another pillow neatly on the bed.

"Well, I guess we'll find out eventually," he responded. I nodded.

"I guess so..."

I hadn't really given much thought to the idea of being pregnant. To be honest, I wasn't sure what to expect if I was. Tamra has always made comments just for the heck of it, but what if she was right? I was unsure if I'd been showing any signs or not; plus, I'd just had my period two weeks prior. A lot of doubt filled my mind at the possibility of being pregnant. Anthony and I have A LOT of sex, but we haven't been actively trying to conceive. We'd just been enjoying each other.

"Alright, let's go do the next room," I said putting the final décor pillow on the bed.

"A'ight."

About twenty minutes later, our doorbell rang, and excitement instantly filled my body. I sat on the couch as Anthony went to answer the door.

"Wassup, bro," was all I heard from Anthony. I stood up and walked towards the door to find Tamra and Raynah standing with their men.

"Hey, girl!" Raynah exclaimed. I opened my arms and embraced them in a group hug. It still warms my heart that I'm so close to them after meeting them when we were all 18 years old. Besides Alana, they're the closest girlfriends I have, and I'm so blessed to have built a lifelong bond with them. Anthony gaining two lifelong friends out of this connection was the icing on the cake.

We walked over to the couch talking amongst ourselves and the guys followed us halfway before stopping by the stairs.

"Baby, I'm about to help them take their stuff upstairs," Anthony told me. I nodded and smiled. After the men disappeared engaging in their own conversation, Tamra looked at me and smirked.

"Girl... You are glowing," she said examining my face. Raynah nodded and smiled extensively. I snickered.

"If that's your way of asking about my skincare routine, you could've just asked," I joked. Tamra rolled her eyes and shot me the middle finger making me laugh.

"Heffa, you know that's not what I mean."

I nodded, "Yeah, I know. But I am not pregnant."

Raynah shook her head and quickly sipped the bottled water that she brought with her.

"I'on know, girly... If I know anything about that man upstairs, it's the fact that I know he eats you alive every chance he gets. There is a high chance you are pregnant."

"O.M.G. ...," I sighed exasperated from this conversation. A slight smile spread across my lips. "I will literally take a test just to prove to you guys that I'm not pregnant. Alright?"

Tamra squealed and clapped her hands.

"Let's go to the store," Raynah suggested. I sighed and nodded. I was truthfully only doing this so they could leave me alone about it. And I wanted to prove that they had absolutely no idea what they were talking about.

***

45 minutes later

"Well... What does it say?" Raynah asked with anticipation through the door. I had to admit that I was a little nervous which is why I decided to do it alone while they sat in my room and waited for my results. I was not prepared for a positive test. My hands were slightly sweaty as I held the digital test in my hand. Apparently, this was one of the most accurate tests that even tells how far along you are. I took a long, deep, steady breath before looking down at the test.

Positive (+) (6 weeks pregnant).

My jaw dropped. I was speechless.

"Kyrah?" Raynah called softly. I stood up and opened the door still in shock. They stared at me waiting for me to say something... but I couldn't. Instead, I just held it out for them to see.

"Oh my! Kyrah... Oh my, God...," Tamra drifted off. She wiped the tears that escaped as she looked at me with love and admiration. Tears formed in my eyes with a smile extending on my lips.

"Oh my God... I'm pregnant..." I said softly. The first words I'd spoken since I first read the test.

"Let's go tell Anthony," Raynah said sniffing with a few tears falling. One of the reasons I love having them as friends is because they share the emotions I feel. Their happiness for me was evident in this moment and I couldn't have asked for better friends.

I nodded and wiped my face. The three of us walked down the hallway to the guest room where all the fellas were hanging out. Anthony looked at me and beamed. My feet instantly walked towards him. A puzzled expression covered his face as he diverted his eyes from me to my friends who were still shedding some tears. My eyes watered as I looked at him.

"Baby, what's wrong?" he asked, concern dripping from his words. Without words, I held up the test for him to see. He frowned a little before his mouth formed an "o".

"Kyrah... Are you...? —" I nodded with tears escaping my eyes. "Oh my God! Baby!" He quickly stood up and embraced me so tenderly. The tears kept flowing and I couldn't stop them. He showered me with kisses, repeatedly calling me beautiful. Happiness filled my heart, and nothing could take this moment away from us.

Chapter Nine

JOY... (ANTHONY'S THOUGHTS)

Everybody has been showering us with love after finding out about the pregnancy. We called our parents who started planning their visit right away. Our friends have been planning names and have started buying things for the baby while they're here. But the whole time, I can't take my eyes off Kyrah. I didn't even think she could ever get more beautiful, but here she is looking more stunning than ever before as she's sitting on the couch with Tamra and Raynah. I continuously watch her as she glows when she smiles at her friends as they talk about baby names and how they hope it's a girl. With how beautiful my wife is, I hope it's a girl, too.

I sat on our back porch with the guys, leaving the girls to talk and hang out. Sean handed me a beer and I opened it.

"Bro... You finna be somebody's daddy," Tommy said before sipping his own drink.

I chuckled. "I already got somebody calling me Daddy," I joked. We all laughed, and Sean shook his head.

"You ain't got no sense, man."

I laughed some more before responding. "Honestly, I can't believe it. But I'm so happy." One of Sean's brows raised.

"You not scared at all?"

I shook my head as I stared off into the evening sky, thinking for a second. I diverted my eyes back to them and smirked a little.

"Nah, not at all. You know, we've been through a lot together. I think this was the news we needed while transitioning into our own family. And I wouldn't want to do this with anybody else. She's the best thing that's ever happened to me... And now she's carrying the next best thing. I don't even feel fear. I just feel... joy."

Tommy fake sniffed and wiped the invisible tears from his eyes.

"That's beautiful, man."

I rolled my eyes and laughed. "Chill out, bruh."

"Nah, for real, man... I'm happy for y'all. If anybody deserves this, it's definitely you. Kyrah's been like my lil' sis since I met her in college. She's a beautiful soul. I ain't gon' lie, I wanted to beat yo ass after everything went down when y'all dated the first time," Sean said before chuckling.

I laughed and nodded completely understanding where he was coming from. That year was rough, but it had to happen so I could learn how to be a better man for Kyrah.

"But", he continued, "I'm thankful that we were able to build our own friendship... hell, a brotherhood thanks to our ladies' close relationship. Anyway... I'm proud of you, man. Congratulations."

"Yeah, bro... Congratulations. You a good dude. You deserve this," Tommy chimed in.

I bit my lip fighting the tears that threatened to spill out. I've never really had consistent friends like Sean and Tommy. Despite what anyone thought, it was often hard for me to connect with people. I've been screwed over too many times before, so I've spent a lot of time keeping to myself with many acquaintances. But ever since I officially met Sean and Tommy after Kyrah and I started dating again, they've been like my brothers apart from my biological older brother. It's nice to have people I can genuinely call my friends.

"'Preciate, y'all, for real," I said dapping them up. We all raised our bottles in a toast before taking a sip.

Kyrah climbed into the bed with one of my T-shirts on and a pair of my boxers. I laughed as I watched her get comfortable beside me. She frowned slightly.

"What'd I do?" she asked puzzled.

I shook my head, "Nothing. Are your clothes too small already?"

She rolled her eyes and laughed. "Now don't be acting like I don't wear your clothes to sleep in on the regular. They're just comfortable. I'll be wearing them a lot more in the future, anyway." I smiled as I pulled her into my arms to cuddle her. She let out a soft sigh as she nuzzled into my chest.

"Anthony?" she said softly.

"Mhm?"

"Do you think we're ready to be parents?"

A slow exhale left my body. This was a question I'd asked myself, but answered as quickly as I'd thought it.

"Absolutely." She looked up at me and smiled.

"Me, too. Thank you for leaving your children in me."

A loud laugh fell from my lips making her laugh, too. Ever since we got married, I'd seen a side of Kyrah that I absolutely loved. She's less timid, and freer. I can't help but think that this is who she had always been but felt she couldn't express herself like this before we got married. And I respected that so much. Every day I felt honored to be able to call myself her husband. She showed me a love I never knew existed and I knew from the moment we first spoke that she would be the one to change my life forever. I lightly smacked her on the butt, and she yelped in response.

"Go to sleep, Kyrah. You sayin' some outlandish stuff," I said still laughing a little.

She giggled. "Goodnight, I love you."

"I love you, too, baby."

Chapter Ten

The week with our friends went by way too fast. It truly warmed my heart that my friends came all this way just to hang out with us and help us settle into our new home. It was even more special having them with us as we discovered the new addition to our new family. We all decided to get some brunch before they had to leave us the next day.

"I'm gonna hate leaving you guys. I wish we could stay longer," Tamra said before placing a fork full of mashed potatoes into her mouth.

"Yeah, me too... especially now that we know y'all are preggo," Raynah said. I chuckled and sighed.

"I know. You guys have to come back, or we'll have to visit home one of these days."

"We will," Anthony said as he placed a hand on my thigh and smiled. I leaned over and kissed him on the cheek. We all enjoyed each other's company as we ate our last meal together before they left for the airport.

Once we got back to the house, their Lyft ride to the airport had arrived. We all stood on our porch embracing one another.

"Let us know when you guys land," I said before they walked away.

"Will do! See you guys soon," Sean said. Anthony and I stood on the porch and watched our friends drive off.

Anthony and I settled onto the couch after coming back into the house. I rested in his arms as my brain created future scenarios of what it would be like to hold our baby in my arms. All the exciting "what ifs" crossed my mind, like what would the baby look like? Who would they resemble most? Will it be a boy or a girl? Will I be a good mom? I closed my eyes trying to visualize how our lives were was about to change in the next almost 8 months.

"I found a midwife and made my first appointment for when I turn 8 weeks," I said breaking the peaceful silence between us.

"Why so long from now?" Anthony asked holding me in his arms. I loved listening to his heartbeat. It was calming.

I shrugged. "I think they can't really see anything or hear a heartbeat before then. According to the nurse, it's normal to be seen around 8 weeks."

"That makes sense. I did mean to ask you about your period, though… I thought you had one a few weeks ago?"

"Oh yeah, remember when I told you it wasn't as heavy as it usually is, and it didn't last that long?" He nodded waiting for me to finish. "Apparently that was not my period. It was something called implantation spotting. The egg was making itself comfortable in my uterus."

He chuckled. "Damn. That makes sense, too." I smiled and leaned into him more. "Well, I can't wait… But in the meantime, I'm hungry… what are you craving?"

I laughed, "Anthony Jamal... Do not use my cravings to start eating all crazy."

"You gon' love this dad-bod," he joked.

I shook my head. "I will love you regardless, you know that."

"Exactly, so what we eatin'?"

I shrugged before thinking. "I don't know... I could go for a sub sandwich."

"Say no more." He kissed the top of my head before he pulled his phone out to order our food.

I was walking around one of the guest rooms, trying to visualize where we could put a crib, a changing table, and everything else the baby would need. Ever since I found out about the baby, it's all I can think about. It consumed my mind and made me excited to start buying things for the baby. Slowly my brain started coming up with ideas and color patterns that could be neutral for either gender. A smile spread across my face as I looked around.

"Hey, baby. I'm about to go to the store to get some things for the house. You wanna come?" Anthony said walking in. I sat on the bed and sighed.

"Nah, I think I'll stay here. I'm coming up with ideas for the nursery."

He chuckled and leaned down to kiss me on the forehead.

"Okay. I'll be right back. Call me if you need me." I smiled and nodded as I watched him disappear out of the room.

My body started to feel slightly tired from all the thinking. I lay down and closed my eyes for a little bit. Suddenly I felt like I was peeing on myself, so I hopped out of the bed. I ran to the bathroom to relieve myself. A low hum came from my lips until I looked down to find red in my underwear. My heart thumped. I wasn't prepared for any of this. I wiped and saw even more blood on the tissue... Too much blood. Tears immediately welled in my eyes. *God... Please, no...*

"Anthony?" I called out knowing he hadn't left yet.

"Yeah?" he called back. A soft sob filled my chest making it hard to form any more words. I heard his footsteps getting closer. My eyes met his as he stopped in his tracks.

"Baby..." he said softly. The tears fell. The cry escaped. I wasn't naïve. I knew exactly what was happening. And nothing or no one could've prepared me for this.

The ride to the emergency room was silent. Fear and grief filled the air. The only comfort my brain would accept was Anthony holding my hand... even then, I couldn't stop the tears. We pulled into the parking lot and quickly headed inside the hospital.

"Hi, how may I help you?" the receptionist asked.

"I'm having a miscarriage", I flatly responded. The cramps were becoming unbearable. The bleeding wouldn't stop. I could feel it spilling from my body. There was no mistaking what this was.

She frowned slightly and nodded, "Okay, hun. Just fill out this paperwork and we'll have you seen as soon as possible."

Anthony took the clipboard, thanked the receptionist, and guided me to a secluded corner. We sat down, both feeling tense.

"Here, lay on my shoulder. I'll fill this out for you," he offered. I cried silently as my head rested on his strong shoulder. Instinctively, I wrapped my arms around my stomach suddenly feeling empty. Our first baby... gone already.

Anthony finished the paperwork and took it back to the receptionist. We waited for a nurse to call me back. There was hardly anyone here so thankfully, I didn't have to wait too long.

"Kyrah?" a voice called. I looked up with puffy eyes to find a nurse standing at the door waiting for us. As we stood up, Anthony softly grabbed my hand and looked at me. A single tear floated down my cheek and he sweetly kissed it away. We followed the nurse to the back ready to face our reality.

***

I lay in our bed, my pillowcase soaked with tears. The happy questions that plagued my mind earlier in the day were replaced with confusion. I closed my eyes, hoping this was a nightmare... but again, I'm not naïve. A soft sob fell from my lips. Anthony hesitantly left me to go pick up some things for me from the store, including pain medication. Through all of this, I'm most thankful for Anthony's tender love and care. I didn't want him to leave me, not even for a second. The tears continued to flow, the pain in my heart more prominent than this physical pain. My lips quivered as I tried to say a prayer.

"God... I don't understand... but I trust You..." This was the hardest prayer I've ever had to pray thus far. There was nothing that could help me understand why this was happening, but I guess there was nothing I could do.

Chapter Eleven

HEALING...

It's been three weeks since the miscarriage and every day was getting easier. As time passed, I've been able to accept what happened in pieces... Tiny pieces. At some point, Anthony suggested I call Moriah just to talk and I couldn't turn that down. I needed to talk to someone. This was my second video call with her since the loss and she was making me feel comfortable as she always does.

"Hi, Kyrah. How are you?" she asked sincerely. I straightened up my laptop camera and exhaled slowly. I nodded my head and gave a small, sad smile.

"Hey, Moriah... I'm... okay." She nodded, matching my smile. She never made me feel like I was a hopeless case. Rather, she always encouraged me and reminded me that I could get through anything I faced. This was something I was unsure of, but having the extra support alongside Anthony was very instrumental in my healing process, physically, mentally, and emotionally.

"How has journaling been going for you?" In response, I shrugged as I pulled out my journal that I used to help with the grieving.

"It's been helping... I've been journaling every day. I think I'm finally past the tearful pages." I chuckled a little.

She smiled warmly. "You sound... peaceful."

My mind pondered on that for a second. Was I at peace? Perhaps coming to terms with my reality is what allows me to smile. I also felt slightly hopeful for the future.

"Yeah...," I started. "I would say I've made peace with what has happened. It hasn't been easy at all... but Anthony has been very helpful in making sure I get out of the house. And he keeps me laughing." I smiled at the thought of my amazing husband.

"I can hear it in your voice."

I smiled, "I'm blessed to have him." My voice drifted off as I started thinking about the possibility of conceiving again. That scared me a little.

"Tell me what just happened," Moriah said catching the shift in my mood.

My brain felt scattered while trying to find a response. Lately, I would journal when my brain would get like this and write about how I wanted to be pregnant again, but I was scared the same thing would happen.

"I don't know if I want to get pregnant again..." I finally responded lowly. Moriah let the silence flow for a while.

"It sounds like you're scared."

A tear slipped from one eye, and I quickly wiped it away, nodding.

"Is that a bad thing?"

"Not at all, Kyrah," she quickly answered. "You just experienced something very traumatic. I imagine you are feeling some hesitation now... and that's completely normal. I've been there."

My eyes grew slightly bigger. "You have?"

She smiled a little and nodded. "Yes. I miscarried my second pregnancy. I was terrified to try again…. But I had hope and faith that God could and would bless us with another one. And He did."

That was a lot to take in. Did it increase the small amount of hope I had? A little… but what if God doesn't bless us with another chance? What then?

We ended the session a little while later and I was all talked out. The feeling of depression tried to creep back into my life just like it did in college. I knew I couldn't lie in bed all day, but I really wanted to. The bleeding had stopped long ago, but I could still feel the pain in my heart as a reminder that I'd never get to meet that precious baby. Therapy helped, but it also reminded me of the loss.

God, why did this have to happen to me? Did I do something? Is something wrong with me? The tears came forcefully as I sat on the edge of the bed trying to fight off this depressive spirit.

"Hey, babygirl," I heard the gentle voice of Anthony say. He walked into the room and knelt in front of me. He gently pulled me in for a hug, letting me cry on his shoulder. "It's okay… I'm right here…" he reassured me. He has been so patient with me like he always is. His kind spirit was so comforting. Had I gone through this with anyone else, I'd be a wreck. But there was always something so calming and reassuring about my husband; it's one of my favorite qualities about him.

He pulled away slightly to catch my eye. He searched them before kissing me on the forehead.

"Let's go get some food." I nodded and stood up with him holding my hand.

***

"Hey, hun. I was just calling you to check on you. How are you doing?" Alana asked me over the phone. I was lounging on the couch with my feet in Anthony's lap while he played his game.

I sighed. I hated that question nowadays because I didn't really know how to respond. Some days I was good, other days I was okay, and sometimes I was not okay at all.

"I'm okay," I settled. "Taking it one day at a time. What's new with you?" I asked diverting the conversation to something other than my issue. I didn't really want to talk about it anymore. Anthony had helped me earlier, so I wanted to just not think about it.

"Girl, nothing much, for real. I've been working. You know me," she responded catching the hint. I chuckled.

"Oh yeah, I know you. How's the new job?"

We talked for a little while longer. It helped me get my mind off everything else which I needed. But there was something I needed to talk to Anthony about. My period was due in a few days which made me nervous. The sight of blood might be a trigger and I wasn't sure if I was ready. On top of that, my midwife said that once I got my period, we were clear to try again. Does Anthony want to try again? Would we be successful? I sighed as I leaned my head back on our comfy, fluffy sectional couch. Anthony paused his game and looked at me.

"What's wrong, sweetheart?" My insides melted a little at his affection. My eyes met his, so caring and gentle.

"Are you scared?" I spat out. He bit his bottom lip and nodded his head a little.

"Honestly, yeah..." he responded. We hadn't really talked about how he felt during all of this, and I felt really guilty. But every time I would try to ask him, he would give me a vague answer and say he was fine. I never wanted to push him, but I wanted him to know I was also there for him.

"How are you? Honestly, Anthony?"

He looked down at his lap, took in a deep inhale, and slowly exhaled. His eyes found mine again and smiled sadly.

"I'm okay, baby... I promise. I have grieved in my own way... but I know that we will get our chance one day. Right now, my focus is on you and making sure you're okay. So, when you ask me if I'm scared, I am, but for a different reason than you are."

I frowned slightly, unsure of what he meant. He pursed his lips before responding and sighed.

"I'm scared you will get depressed again... I can't stand to see you like that." For the first time, I saw pure fear in his eyes. This whole time, he'd allowed himself to grieve the loss of our baby, but he was especially concerned about my mental health.

"Baby..." I responded.

"Kyrah, baby..." he held out his hand for me to place mine in. He held it gently as he looked into my eyes. "You have no idea how much it breaks me to see you like that and there's absolutely nothing I can do to make you feel better but be here for you. Yes, I am sad about losing our baby... but, Kyrah, if I ever lost you, I don't know what I would do... So, when I tell you I'm okay, I really am okay. I just have to make sure you're okay, too."

I wiped the tears that escaped while listening to his loving words. They penetrated my heart, making me wonder how I ever got so lucky to end up with this man.

"But to answer your initial question", he continued, "no, I'm not scared. I'm ready whenever you're ready to try again. But we'll go at your pace, a'ight?"

I smiled and nodded, "Okay."

Chapter Twelve

Try Again...

I looked up from my journal and stared out our bedroom window as I sat on our bed, legs crossed and back against the headboard. Anthony had gone to work so I was here by myself, in the quiet. A small sigh fell from my lips. My phone vibrated, zoning me back into reality. Kyla. My sister's face appeared on the screen.

"Hey, sis," I said answering the video call.

"Hey, sissy. How are you?" she replied.

I shrugged and smiled a little. "I'm good. A little bored. Waiting for Anthony to come back home."

She laughed, "Y'all are inseparable."

I rolled my eyes playfully. "No, he's attached to me," I joked.

"Girl, please," she responded still laughing. I chuckled. "Anyway, I was calling to see if you guys were planning to come down for my mom & dad's anniversary party. I'm finalizing the guest list right now."

"Yeah, we should be there. It's in two weeks, right?" She nodded. Before I could respond, Anthony walked in looking fine as ever. I smiled.

"Your husband must've just walked in", Kyla said in an amused yet sarcastic tone. I laughed and nodded. He looked at me and smirked before sitting beside me on the bed.

"Hello to you, too, Kyla," he said jokingly.

"Hey, bro. I was just calling to confirm if you guys are coming to the anniversary party for Mom and Dad."

He paused and thought about it for a second. A deep exhale left his body as he face-palmed.

"I don't think I can go," he finally said. The way I frowned so quickly, it would seem like he insulted me.

"What?" I responded. His eyes met mine and without words, I caught the hint that we needed to talk.

"Sis, I'll call you back with a final answer," I told Kyla.

"Okay, sis. Bye." I hung up the phone and looked at Anthony waiting for an explanation. So many questions swam through my head. *Why hadn't he mentioned this before? Did he expect me to fly alone? Not the way my anxiety is set up.* I cleared my throat still waiting for him to say something... anything.

"Anthony, what happened?"

He sighed. "Baby, I'm so sorry. I have to stay here for an HR convention that weekend. I just found out today. I completely forgot about your parents' party and told them I'd be there."

My eyes closed in frustration. Although I knew the chances of something like this happening were great, the frustration came from him not remembering that we were supposed to go home after already planning. Our families couldn't visit us after the miscarriage, so we made plans to go to them instead. I missed them. I missed home.

"Anthony… what the hell…" I said exasperated. I got out of the bed and walked towards the bathroom. He followed me into the bathroom and stood at the door while I relieved myself.

"Baby, I'm sorry," he said defeated as he shoved his hands in his pockets.

"I know… I know… I just…" I drifted off for a second. "I was just looking forward to going home and seeing everybody." I stood up from the toilet and stood in front of the sink to wash my hands. Anthony walked up behind me, wrapping his arms around my waist.

"You can still go."

I shook my head. "You know I hate flying alone. I'd rather drive… and I would if it wasn't so far."

He chuckled, "I know you would. Let me see what I can do, a'ight? And if I can't back out, I'll make it up to you, I promise." He kissed the side of my neck and I smiled.

"Have I ever told you how beautiful you are?" he asked seductively, still planting sweet kisses on my neck. I giggled and turned around to face him with his arms still around me.

"You'll have to refresh my memory," I responded with a sly smile. His bottom lip was between his teeth as he leaned down to kiss me slowly.

"Hm… your beauty is drivin' me crazy…" His Atlanta accent was coming out, making me weak in the knees. "I've been thinkin' 'bout you all day…" His large hands slowly roamed my body gaining a response out of me. I sighed in ecstasy.

"Listen to me," he sternly, yet softly demanded gaining all my attention. His eyes flickered between my lips and my eyes before finally landing on my eyes. I couldn't look away even if I wanted to. He frowned in what looked to be sexual frustration which I completely understood and related to in this moment. He pulled one of the straps on my camisole off my shoulder and left soft kisses starting from my shoulder blade up to my jaw. My eyes closed in response, waiting for his next move.

"Don't hold back tonight. I want you to be as loud as you can be," his deep voice finally rumbled, sending chills throughout my body.

A light moan escaped my lips as he picked me up. I wrapped my legs around his torso with my lips connected to his. He carried me back to our bed and laid me down, still kissing me slowly. Layer by layer, he peeled my clothes off before removing his. My eyes closed in pleasure, moans and groans escaping both of us once our bodies connected.

He grunted into my neck as he made sweet, slow love to me. The way he touched me and kissed me in hidden places was calculated. He always knew exactly what to do to get me to the highest point of pleasure. I appreciated the time he's taken to learn my body and what I enjoy by closely paying attention to how my body responds. It was always perfect.

Our eyes connected briefly, taking this to another level. His beautiful long locs hung loosely on either side of his handsome face. He leaned down and kissed me deeply, further solidifying our special union.

I woke up the next morning in Anthony's arms. *Gotta pee.* Slowly, I slipped from his arms, careful not to wake him up. A chuckle slipped from my lips as I listened to him snore. I walked into the bathroom when my eyes glanced at the drawer that held a few pregnancy tests. I'd bought more a while ago but never wanted to take them out of fear. Fear of a negative test and fear of a positive test. At this point, I wasn't sure how I would respond to either result.

"Oh, why not?" I said lowly. Obviously, the sex from last night wasn't going to give me a positive test, but we'd been having sex a lot lately. There was a 50/50 chance that I could already be pregnant.

I opened a digital test that could give pregnancy results about 5 days before a missed period. My period was due the next day so I figured I might as well prepare for Mother Nature by seeing a negative result.

After taking the test, I placed it on the counter and waited for the results as I cleaned myself up and washed my hands. I admittedly avoided looking at it because I feared what it might say. I was secretly hoping it was a defective one so I could just toss it and say, "I tried". A deep sigh rose in my chest.

"Here goes nothing..." I said under my breath. My eyes scanned the small screen. *Positive (+) (3 weeks).* Tears immediately welled in my eyes, but I wasn't sure if they were tears of joy. A mix of emotions plagued me; so many thoughts entered my mind. I was more afraid than anything. Suddenly the bathroom door opened, and Anthony appeared from behind.

"Hey," he said in his sleepy voice. "I was wonderin' where you went." He walked over to me, kissing me on the cheek. His eyes moved from mine to the pregnancy test on the counter. I saw his eyebrows raise and a small smile grow on his face. I wish I could match that smile.

"Baby..." he said happily. Tears streamed down my cheeks. His smile was immediately replaced with slightly furrowed brows. "What's going on?" he asked.

"Anthony... I'm scared." Without hesitation, he pulled me into his chest and embraced me. I let the tears flow. I allowed myself to feel. I couldn't fake the happiness because the fear was too prominent. Fearful thoughts overwhelmed me, especially with it being so early in the pregnancy. And now I can't help but wonder if I'll lose this baby, too.

Chapter Thirteen

After finding out I was carrying another baby again, I knew I needed to talk to Moriah. We had a video call, and she was very understanding. After she briefly shared her miscarriage story with me after my last pregnancy, she made me feel seen. Heard. Understood. So, I knew that she was the person I needed to talk to about everything I'd been feeling surrounding this new pregnancy.

"Moriah, I have been having mixed feelings about this pregnancy. I want to be happy... I really do. But something is blocking me from feeling it," I admitted. I toyed with the ruffled ends of my soft blanket that I had for comfort. Anthony was at work, and I had been stuck in the house alone with my terrorizing thoughts.

"You sound hesitant about allowing yourself to embrace this pregnancy."

I nodded. "Yeah... I am."

"Let's explore that some more—the hesitancy."

I took a deep breath and pondered on what exactly was going on through my mind. If my thoughts were butterflies, I'd need a net to catch them so I could stop them from swarming around my brain. On one end, I could feel Anthony's joy and happiness behind all of this. Part of me was jealous that I couldn't feel that, too. Why wouldn't my brain let me feel that?

"I don't know if I can handle another miscarriage," I finally blurted out. "It was too much for me. There was nothing that could've prepared me for that. And now I feel like I'm walking on eggshells around this. I'm scared."

She nodded, thinking of her response. "Try to name what you're scared of."

"I'm scared that if I allow myself to get comfortable with this... if I let myself fully accept this, I will lose it again..."

That was the only explanation I could think of. There was no other reason for me to be scared besides the fact that history would repeat itself.

"Kyrah, you sound a lot like me. I get exactly where you're coming from. But I want to encourage you to have hope. This is a blessing. You deserve this blessing, okay?"

I nodded trying to... wanting to believe whatever she was saying. It was to the point where I was running out of tears to cry. I just wanted the baby to be okay.

***

Two Weeks Later

"You all packed up, babygirl?" Anthony asked as he was spraying on his cologne that I loved oh so much. I was going down my list of essentials that I would need for the trip home. Anthony was able to pull some strings and find a replacement. He told them that he had to fly home for a family emergency. I'd say that's accurate. Either way, I was glad we were able to take this trip.

"Mhm," I replied with a smile.

He smirked and walked over to me, wrapping his arms around me. His lips found my jaw leaving light, but damp kisses on my skin. I giggled.

"Anthony, stop it."

"You always look so damn good... especially when we have to leave the house."

I laughed, "Well, unfortunately for you, we don't have time for a quickie. We literally have to go."

He groaned and pulled away, smacking his lips. "I guess."

"Listen, I gotcha when we get to the hotel tonight. I promise." I looked down at my phone and saw that our Lyft driver was about 2 minutes away. "Our ride's almost here."

He sighed, "A'ight. Let's go." He had a playful, pitiful look on his face that made me laugh. I stood on my tippy toes and kissed him on the cheek.

"My little horn-ball," I teased. He smacked me on the butt making me laugh. We started grabbing our things and headed downstairs. Our Lyft driver pulled up as soon as we placed our things by the front door. I offered to carry some of the heavier bags, but Anthony wasn't having it. I stepped outside and hopped in the car, waiting for Anthony and the driver to finish putting our things in the trunk. As soon as they got in the car, we were off to the airport.

I couldn't wait to go home. Being in a familiar environment was sure to lift my spirits and bring me the comfort I'd been searching for. I just wanted to be around family and friends. Anthony was always enough, but I could tell we both needed this. The way he was adamant about pulling some strings to be able to take this trip was heartwarming and it meant a lot to me. He is the sweetest thing that has ever happened to me and now that we're pregnant again, it deepens my love for him.

The plane ride was not bad at all. It didn't take long for us to find our bags and get out of that busy airport. As soon as we walked out of the door, Kyrie was standing there waiting for us with his girlfriend, Arianna.

"Wassup, y'all!" he greeted us. He gave me a big hug and I let myself feel the emotions that surfaced. As much as we would go back and forth, I missed him.

"Hey, bro," I said with tears in my eyes.

"I know you not cryin'", he joked as he pulled away. I wiped my face and laughed.

"Leave me alone," I responded in between laughs. I hadn't shared the news of the pregnancy, yet so I didn't want to tell him that it was my hormones making me extra emotional. He shook his head and chuckled before he dapped up Anthony.

"Wassup, bro."

"Wassup, man," Anthony responded. I hugged Arianna and smiled at her.

"It's nice to see you," I said.

She smiled widely, "You, too!" Anthony and Kyrie put our bags in the trunk, and we all piled into the car. Like always, Anthony grabbed my hand and held it the whole way home to Augusta.

Anthony and I were finally able to settle into our hotel room after the long ride. We opted out of going to see everyone since we would see them at the party tomorrow. And truthfully, I was feeling pretty exhausted. Although I was only about five weeks pregnant, I could feel the symptoms of it, and right now, lying down sounded like the best thing in the world.

"You tired, baby?" Anthony asked as I rested my head on his chest.

"Yeah, a little. I just wanna lay here."

"Need some help going to sleep?" he teased.

I giggled, "Hm...", I sat up and looked at his amused expression. "Since you're offering, I might take you up on that."

He smirked, slowly leaning in to kiss me. I giggled into the kiss and positioned myself on his lap. There was no denying the fact that I couldn't get enough of this man. I always wanted him, and I loved that he always wanted me. I especially enjoyed the times like this one when we could be silly and playful while fulfilling each other's needs. There was something so intimate and sweet about our expression of love for one another that couldn't be replicated. I can never begin to imagine this feeling with anyone else, and I am so blessed to be able to start a family with him.

He planted small kisses on my collarbone making me giggle from the ticklish feeling. A smile lit up his face before his lips met mine. My body was on fire from the pleasure. I did my best not to disturb the rooms around us, but I'm sure my efforts were wasted.

After about an hour of lovemaking, we lay in the bed cuddling, listening to each other breathe. He drew light circles on my back, soothing me into a tempting sleep.

"I think I was too loud," I said amused.

He chuckled, "You were holding back."

"I didn't wanna disturb anybody."

He smacked his lips, "They would've been a'ight."

I laughed, "Boy..." He laughed and kissed me on the head. "Anyway, are you happy to be home?"

He exhaled, "I am. I think we both really need this escape, especially after everything that's happened. I know our moms will be happy to lay eyes on you."

I smirked and snuggled closer to him. "Yeah, I know. I don't know if I want to tell anyone about this pregnancy, yet."

"Then we won't tell'em, a'ight?" he kissed me on the top of my head, making me smile in gratitude for him. He kept drawing small circles on my back soothing me to sleep.

Chapter Fourteen

We pulled up to the party venue and were quickly greeted by our family. Everyone was so happy and surprised to see us walk in. And as we decided, we didn't tell anybody about our pregnancy. One of the main reasons I didn't want to tell anyone is because I didn't want to answer any questions, yet. Also, I didn't want to get too excited. There was still a small part of me that was scared of this pregnancy going wrong. I knew I needed to be more positive about it because I'm also aware that the baby can feel everything I'm feeling. But I just didn't want to get my hopes up. And talking about it would do just that.

Seeing family that I hadn't seen in years truly lifted my spirits. We all danced and took pictures like we always do when we get together. Feeling tired from all the dancing and socializing, I headed to the drink table to grab a bottle of water. My eyes scanned the room to find Anthony talking and laughing with his dad and my dad. A smile grew on my face while watching the interaction.

"Your husband is so handsome," one of my aunts, Marla, said walking up to me with another aunt. I chuckled.

"Don't tell him that. It'll make his head bigger," I joked.

She laughed and shook her head. "I don't mean to pry, but are you two having babies any time soon? They would be so beautiful."

"Oh, yes! They would be absolutely adorable," my other aunt, Sheri chimed in.

Aunt Marla nodded, "You two aren't getting any younger. I say you go ahead and get started." Aunt Sheri giggled and nodded. My heart immediately dropped listening to their banter, and I tried my best to hide it. I didn't exactly know how to respond to that. Was it really any of their business? And honestly, this whole exchange felt a little insensitive. *I'm trying to have babies... but I haven't been able to... And I already feel guilty about it...* I shrugged and put on a fake smile wanting to be respectful.

"We're just enjoying being married right now," I responded.

Aunt Sheri wiggled her eyebrows and nodded with a smirk, "Oh, I understand that."

I cleared my throat, "Excuse me for a moment." I quickly walked away without looking back to find somewhere to get fresh air. My feet took me outside on the balcony where I exhaled as soon as the air hit my lungs. I knew this was bound to happen. I knew the moment I saw distant family members; someone would ask about children. But even then, I still wasn't prepared. A sigh left my lips as I fought the tears that threatened to escape. This pregnancy was scary. And no one besides Anthony even knew about it.

"Hey, what's going on?" I heard a familiar voice say from behind. I quickly patted my eyes dry and turned around to face my mom.

"Ma'am, you should be inside. It's your party," I said with a slight chuckle.

She shrugged, "None of that matters right now. Are you okay?" She walked towards me and looked into my eyes.

I shook my head. "Aunty Marla asked me when we were having children... I didn't really know how to respond."

My mom chuckled and shook her head. "That Marla... As sweet as she is, she is nosy, isn't she?" I laughed and nodded.

"Listen, sweetie," she continued, "I know we didn't get to come see you guys after the announcement and after the miscarriage. But I am so happy to see you two. And not that you need to hear this from me, but you guys go at your own pace... including the grieving. Losing a baby is never easy, you know I know that." I nodded as tears slipped from my eyes. My mom rarely talked about her experience with the loss of my baby sisters. Hearing her open up about it was comforting even though I could never understand the extent of loss the way she did.

It was a touchy subject and something none of us expected. Yet, my mom always seemed to handle it with grace. She never complained and she always kept her faith in God. However, now that I'm going through my own personal loss, I can't imagine she didn't have questions or even moments of doubt.

"Can I ask you a question, Mom?" She nodded and waited for me to continue. "How did you do it? How did you keep trusting God after? Because I'm having a really tough time."

She gave a small smile and grabbed one of my hands, holding it tenderly.

"I had my moments of anger and doubt. I didn't understand why God allowed it to happen." A look of surprise showed on my face, and she chuckled. "But I just talked to Him, no matter what I was feeling. And I was honest about what I felt even when I didn't feel like talking to him." [*That sounds like what Moriah has been telling me since college*.] "I want you to be encouraged in this time and know that everything is going to be okay... you will be okay. I promise." She pulled me in for an embrace and I allowed myself to feel like "little Kyrah" who needed her mommy for a moment. She gently rubbed my back consoling me.

"Now, let's go dance before they kick us out," she said as she pulled away slightly to wipe my tears. I nodded and smiled. We linked our arms together and walked back inside the building.

I stood in front of the mirror in our hotel bathroom cleaning the makeup off my face. I pulled my hair up in a puff and sighed ready to get in the bed. My eyes scanned down to my stomach trying to imagine it bigger than what it is. I've always had a little belly, but I was very curious to see what it would look like if I was pregnant with a big belly. A small smile grew on my face as I started to feel the slightest bit of hope. Anthony walked in with his glass on and his locs in a low bun.

"What you doin'?" he asked with a smirk.

I groaned and chuckled lowly. "I'm just looking at myself. Trying to picture myself pregnant."

He smiled, "I can't wait to see you like that, not gonna lie."

I turned towards him. "You just want to see me waddle around with swollen ankles and feet." He moved closer to me and smiled.

"Exactly. And I can't wait to rub your belly and kiss it."

"And the baby kicks?" I squealed a little.

He chuckled, "And the baby kicks." He placed a hand on my stomach and smiled. I placed my hand on top of his returning the smile. The smile on my face suddenly dropped as I recalled the conversation with my aunts.

"Do you think the miscarriage was my fault?" I asked him lowly. He closed his eyes for a moment, taking a deep breath. His eyes met mine.

"No, baby. There is nothing you did to cause that, okay? Please don't think like that."

I sighed in exhaustion. I'd been carrying this guilt around for a while, blaming myself. Maybe I didn't drink enough water or something... anything.

"Let's go to bed," he said removing his hand and holding it out for me to grab. I placed my hand in his and followed him to bed.

Chapter Fifteen

March 26th, 2021

I beamed as I stood in the mirror getting ready for my first appointment with my midwife. She was so excited to finally see me again, especially after my last pregnancy. With the pandemic still going on, we had to take extra precautions like making sure we had face masks for the appointment. Thankfully, Anthony was able to take the afternoon off work to come with me. Just as I was putting my earrings on, I heard him come into the house and make his way upstairs.

"Hey, baby, you ready?" he asked as he walked in, kissing me on the cheek.

"Hey, almost. I just need to grab my things." We both walked into the bedroom so I could get my purse and phone. "Okay, I'm ready. Do you have masks in the car?"

He nodded, "Yep." I smiled and followed him all the way out of the house.

I really expected to be a nervous wreck on the way to the appointment, but I was finally feeling excited and hopeful. Anthony told me about his day and how he was glad to get the rest of the day off. He also promised that after the appointment, we would go on a lunch date that he'd planned a few days ago.

We arrived at the hospital and went to the floor where the Midwives' office was. After filling out the paperwork, we patiently waited in the waiting area for my name to be called. I couldn't wait to hear the baby's heartbeat. I felt like this day would never come...

"Kyrah?" A nurse called out. We stood up and followed her to the back. She took my vitals and asked me the usual questions. Everyone here was so nice, and I couldn't wait to go through this journey with them on my team.

"You ready?" Anthony asked as we sat in the examining room waiting for my midwife. A wide smile spread across my lips.

"I am. Finally feeling hopeful." He smiled as he grabbed one of my hands and kissed the back of it. Like clockwork, there was a knock on the door and it opened shortly after. In walked a cute, bubbly, fair-skinned woman with super curly hair.

"Hi, Kyrah. It's so nice to finally see you again", she greeted as she sanitized her hands.

"Hi, Sarah. It's nice to finally see you again, too."

She smiled and looked at Anthony, "You must be daddy."

He smirked and leaned back, "Well—" I lightly hit him on the arm while laughing. Sarah chuckled and nodded.

"Hey, that's how we got here, right?"

"Exactly," Anthony said with a smirk still on his face.

My face burned as I face-palmed from slight embarrassment. *I can't take this man anywhere.* We laughed. Sarah sat down on the stool in front of me and beamed.

"Well, I know you guys are ready to hear a heartbeat so let's get to that, shall we?" I smiled in response, excited to move on. We went over the formalities like the start day of my last period, my symptoms, and even my concerns with this pregnancy.

"Alright, guys. I think we can listen to this baby," she said enthusiastically. She instructed me to lay back and pulled out the vaginal ultrasound.

"Just relax. I'm gonna put some gel on this to make it more comfortable so we can find baby." I nodded and took a deep breath. Anthony held his hand out for me to hold. He was always here to comfort me in uncomfortable moments.

"Okay, here we go," Sarah said. She slowly put the probe in and the screen showed the inside of my uterus. Wow. Sarah took her time explaining where everything was so we wouldn't be confused. I glanced over at Anthony and saw him mesmerized. I chuckled.

"And there's baby," she squealed. Tears welled in my eyes from seeing the tiny baby on the screen.

"Let's try to get this heartbeat."

We waited for the sound, but we didn't hear anything. Panic settled in my chest as she tried to find the heartbeat with no luck. Anthony squeezed my hands when he saw the horrific look on my face.

She pulled the probe out slowly and pulled the gloves off her hands. A slight frown etched her brows.

"I will be right back, guys," she said softly before walking out of the room.

The room was quiet. Both Anthony and I were lost in our personal thoughts. I wish I knew what he was thinking. Fear filled my brain and my heart. Anthony turned his gaze to me, meeting my watery eyes.

"Baby, I love you, okay? You are so strong." I listened to his words, but nothing was comforting me right now. I'm tired of this. I don't want to do this anymore. The tears streamed down my face uncontrollably.

"Anthony…" was all I could say before a soft sob left my chest. The door opened and Sarah walked back in with another nurse. I tried to get myself together. They tried to console me. I tried to listen to what they had to say. But I heard nothing. I just felt… empty.

I sat silently in the passenger seat on the way home. There was nothing anyone could say or do to make this better. We walked into the house quietly. Bitterness filled my heart as tears poured from my eyes. The pain in my stomach kept reminding me that we'd just suffered another painful loss.

For the remainder of the evening, I sat in the guestroom that was going to be the nursery and stared out the window. I had no appetite. I just wanted to be left alone. The overwhelming feeling of depression was taking over, and I was letting it. There was no use in fighting it anymore. I couldn't pretend like I was hopeful or trusted God in this anymore. There was nothing left. I had nothing left to give.

Anthony walked into the room and eyed me softly. I looked at him noticing he was looking back at me with pain in his own eyes.

"Kyrah, you need to eat something."

"I'm not hungry."

He sighed. "At least come out of this room. You can't stay in here, baby."

I shrugged and looked back out of the window. It was silent for a few moments before Anthony's heartbreaking tone broke it.

"Babygirl, talk to me—"

"I don't wanna talk. I just wanna... I just wanna sit here," I said lowly with angst dripping from every word.

He sighed softly. "Why won't you let me in, Kyrah?" He asked desperately with a slight crack in his voice. I looked at him with tears spilling from my tired, puffy eyes.

"Because I'm angry!" I broke down. My heart shattered. I could feel my body becoming numb, ready to give out. A painful sob fell from my lips. "I just don't understand..." I cried out.

Instead of responding with words, Anthony responded with pure love. He walked towards me and wrapped his strong arms around me as he sat by my side. My tears stained his chest as my thoughts plagued me. All I could feel was heavy sorrow in my chest.

"Babygirl... please talk to me," he pleaded, still holding me tight. I sobbed trying to find the words.

"Why won't God let us have a baby?" I desperately cried. I know he didn't have the answer, but it was the only thing that came out. Suddenly I heard him sniffing. I pulled away from him slightly to look at his face. Tears streamed down his beautiful face breaking my heart even more. I selfishly hadn't considered how he was feeling through these miscarriages. Mainly because he never talked about it.

His watery eyes met mine. No words were spoken. They weren't needed. At that moment, we just knew we needed each other to get through this painful loss. Although he couldn't feel it physically, I could see that he was feeling it emotionally no matter how much he tried to hold it together. I reached up and caressed his cheek and he kissed the palm of my hand. Without hesitation, I wrapped my arms around his torso, resting on his chest once again, and he quickly embraced me.

I sighed as more tears came from my eyes.

"Anthony... this hurts," I said softly with a cracked voice.

"I know, baby..." he sniffed and leaned down to kiss me on the forehead. My heart was becoming bitter towards God, and I had a hard time finding the words to say to Him right now. And for the rest of the night, I couldn't do anything else but cry.

Chapter Sixteen

ANTHONY'S PRAYER... (ANTHONY'S THOUGHTS)

She was slowly checking out, and this is what I was afraid of. Witnessing her go through depression in college was very hard. I could never imagine what she was going through, but I did my best to be there for her. And now that it looks like she's going through it again, I am trying to be there for her in the way that she needs me to be.

These losses have affected me, too, but in a different way. It hurts that we haven't been able to have successful pregnancies. Hell, I definitely feel like I'm ready to be a dad. But I'm more affected by how it's distressing my wife. It's clear that she is struggling. I can tell she's probably blaming herself. I just wish she would talk to me.

It's the day after her scheduled D&C. That was rough on her. She tried to be strong through it, but all of this was breaking her which was breaking my heart.

"Babygirl, I have to leave soon," I say as I'm pulling out my clothes for work. I didn't want to leave her here by herself. There was no way

I could get out of work. I already used the family emergency excuse to go home and now I'm regretting it. There was nothing more I wanted than to stay by her side and take care of her. Her tired eyes met mine as I knelt down beside her. She was lying in the bed with tears in her eyes.

"Please don't leave me...", she said almost in a whisper. My head dropped at the feeling of my heartstrings being pulled. The ache in my chest almost made me say "Forget this job" and hop in the bed with her.

"Baby, don't do that..." I pleaded returning my gaze to her.

She sniffed as the tears rolled down. "I don't want to be alone."

"I know... I don't wanna leave you here..." I sighed trying to come up with a solution.

She was still recovering and needed rest. We hadn't made many friends here, yet, so there was no one I could call to come sit with her for a few hours. *I got it*. I placed a hand on her cheek and wiped her tears.

"Let me see if I can work from home the next few days," I suggested.

She nodded and gave a small, tired smile. My heart leaped a little. She hasn't smiled since before the last appointment. I kissed her on the forehead, telling her "Be right back" before standing up to leave the room. I closed the door and leaned against it. I looked up as the tears I'd been holding in since she asked me not to leave fell from my eyes. I hated seeing her like this. I ran my hand down my face, quickly wiping the tears away before walking away from the room to make a phone call. There was no way I was leaving her alone.

My fingers moved fast on my phone to call in my office. After about three rings, my boss picked up. Although I'm a supervisor in HR, I still have someone higher up in the department to answer to.

"Hello?" He answered from the other end.

"Hey, Johnny. I need to request to work from home for the next couple of days."

Without hesitation, he approved the request, transferring my call to the person in charge of documenting workers' time away from the office. The best part about working in the HR department is being able to pull strings when and if I need to without much pushback. I was thankful that Johnny didn't give me a hard time about it. I'm guessing it's mainly because I'll still be working, just not in the office.

"Alright, Teresa. Thank you." I hung up the phone and made my way back to our room. Once I walked in, I saw Kyrah sound asleep, still snuggled under the comforter. I walked over to her and kissed her lightly on the cheek. Her eyes opened a little and she smiled.

"Hey," she said weakly.

"Hey, baby... I talked to my department head. He approved my request to work from home for the next few days so I can stay here with you."

She exhaled in relief and closed her eyes for a second. A light "thank you" came from her lips and I nodded in response.

"I'll be downstairs working. Get some rest. I'll order us some food." I kissed her tenderly. My eyes scanned hers as I pulled away. "I love you."

"I love you, too." I headed downstairs where my laptop and work-bag were to clock in and get started on some work.

Today was worse for Kyrah than the day before. She'd been bleeding and cramping making her recovery hard. I did everything I could to make her more comfortable, but I believe more of the discomfort was emotional. I could only imagine what she was going through internally. I know I lost the babies, too, but she's the one who had to experience the losses both physically and emotionally. And it hurts to know that there's only so much I can do.

***

I had an hour lunch break and decided to go hang out with Kyrah and see how she was doing. As I walked into the room, I saw her fast asleep with her journal lying next to her. This is the first time she's journaled in a while, but she hasn't talked to Moriah, yet. She hasn't talked to anyone. Not to mention, our families don't know about any of this.

A sigh left my chest as I walked closer to her. I didn't want to invade her personal space, but my eyes scanned the page her journal was opened to. I skimmed it and saw something that broke my heart.

I noticed a few tear stains on the page breaking my heart even more. I closed the journal and placed it quietly on her dresser. Crying silent tears have become common for me lately. I climbed into the bed with her and held her. Tears formed in my eyes and a low prayer escaped my lips.

"Lord God... please heal my baby's heart... keep her heart soft towards You... give her peace of mind... Lord, she is hurting, but I know You are the greatest comforter we could ever know... we don't understand any of this... but right now I'm asking You to comfort Kyrah... she needs You more than anything right now..."

There was nothing else I could do but hold her and pray over her as thoughts swam through my head. Why would she even think she wasn't good enough for me? I don't care if we never have kids. I just want her... I want her here with me. I just wish she could see that.

After lying in bed with her for a few minutes, I slowly got up to get ready to get back to work. She shifted and her eyes fluttered open.

"Hey," she said sleepily. I smiled.

"Hey, sweetheart. I was just about to go back downstairs to finish up my work for the day."

She stretched and yawned as she slowly sat up. She briefly looked around before looking at me.

"Okay... I'm gonna shower. Can we go somewhere when you get off?"

My brows rose in surprise. That was the last thing I expected to hear. "Of course. Where you wanna go?"

She shrugged, "Wherever."

I smirked and nodded. "I'll find somewhere. I should be done soon. I took a late lunch, so I'll be done within the next hour or so."

She smiled a little, melting my heart. She is so beautiful. I don't know how I ever got so lucky to be with someone like her. She's the strongest person I've ever met. And I'm glad I get to be here to hold her up when she needs me.

"Okay," she replied. I leaned down and kissed her softly on her lips.

She bit her lip and giggled. My ears grew hot from hearing one of my favorite sounds. I hadn't heard it in what feels like forever. I kissed her one more time before I left the room. I couldn't wait to spend some time with her away from the place that currently holds sad memories.

***

"I'm ready," Kyrah said as she placed her glasses over her eyes. Her beautiful smile caught my attention while I was putting my shoes on.

"You look beautiful," I complimented. She chuckled.

"Babe... stop lyin'." I admired her as she carefully pushed her glasses up on her nose. She doesn't realize how beautiful she is even with just a T-shirt and a pair of leggings on. I smirked as I walked toward her. Her eyes met mine as I placed a hand under her chin.

"What do I always tell you? I'd never lie about your beauty. Even more beautiful with that smile on your face." She blushed and smiled a little. "Come on, let's go."

We headed downstairs and out of the house to go to our destination. Once she asked me if we could go somewhere, I knew immediately where I wanted to take her. There was a nice coffee shop in the downtown area that I found a few weeks ago. I figured she'd want to go one day.

After a fifteen-minute drive downtown, we pulled up to the coffee shop/bookstore called "Books n' Mugs". I glanced over at Kyrah to read her reaction. Her eyebrows raised as her eyes brightened slightly. She looked at me and smiled. I parked the car and opened her door for her as always. We walked inside the small building hand-in-hand, both of us looking around as we took in the ambiance. Soft lo-fi music played in the background as some people sat with books, laptops, and their coffees and snacks.

"How did you find this place?" she asked softly with a smile.

I shrugged. "We needed a new coffee shop for when we get into a disagreement," I joked recalling one of our first arguments in college. She laughed and rolled her eyes.

"Well, looks like we gotta get into an argument to see if it's a match."

"I guess we'll find out," I replied with a smirk.

After we ordered our coffee and bakery snacks, we headed to the books section to get Kyrah a few new books. She easily found some new books that she wanted to read by some of her favorite romance authors. Once we purchased them, we found a secluded table for us to sit with each other. I'd brought my laptop to keep me busy so she could read in peace.

"Feel like arguing, yet?" she asked jokingly. I looked around and shook my head.

"Nah. It's too peaceful in here. I'on think this is our spot, babygirl." She giggled before opening her book. Hearing her laugh lit up my heart. With everything that's been happening with us, it's been a while since I've heard her genuinely laugh. A few moments of silence passed before I broke it.

"Sweetheart," I said softly to get her attention. Her cheeks flushed slightly as she looked up from her book.

"Hm?"

"Are you okay?" I asked sincerely.

I'd been avoiding bringing up the second loss. It's a sensitive topic and the last thing I wanted to do was trigger her. Her shoulders tensed instantly making me regret bringing it up. She pursed her full lips and nodded slowly before shrugging.

I sighed. "I'm sorry... I didn't mean to—"

"Are you okay?" she asked tenderly with tears in her eyes. I reached my hand across the table waiting for her to place her hand in mine. I gently squeezed her hand for reassurance.

"I'm okay... It has been hard... But it's been harder watching how much it's affecting you. I genuinely wish there was more I could do... Something... But I feel helpless," I admitted.

We hadn't talked about me and how I've been feeling. Not because Kyrah never asked but because I didn't feel a need to talk about it. I do want children and I dream of seeing Kyrah pregnant with my child. I want to experience that just like she does. But I didn't want her to have to keep going through this. It's hard watching the person you love the most hurt in a way that there is nothing you can do to make them feel better.

She exhaled slowly. "I'm sorry..."

I frowned, "Babygirl, stop. None of this is your fault." A tear slipped from one of her eyes and she quickly wiped it away.

"I feel like I did something to lose our babies... Something I didn't do right or—"

"Kyrah. Stop." She looked at me with wet cheeks from her tears. I had no idea she'd been blaming herself for these losses. Why would she think that?

I shook my head, holding her gaze. "I'm not letting you apologize for something that you can't control. Okay?"

She nodded while slowly exhaling.

"I love you no matter what."

She cracked a small smile, "I love you, too..." She chuckled a little and sighed. "Not an argument, but I think this is our spot."

I smiled as I intertwined our fingers. "I think so, too."

Chapter Seventeen

Days passed and it was time for me to go back into the office. I didn't want to, but I'd already told Johnny that I only needed a few days at home. A sigh escaped my lips as I pulled my shirt over my head as I was getting ready for work. My eyes met Kyrah's who was silently watching me.

"You okay?" I asked her. She smiled and nodded. "What are you gonna do today?"

She shrugged. "I'm not sure, yet. Maybe read one of those books you bought me the other day." I walked towards her, sitting down by her feet.

"Okay. I know you told me you feel better, physically, but I still want you to take it easy. Don't overdo it."

She chuckled, "Anthony, I'm fine. Hurry up so you're not late. Don't worry about me."

I smirked, "Not a chance."

"Yo, Anthony. Wassup, man? Haven't seen you in a couple of days," one of my colleagues, Bernard, said as he walked up to me in the breakroom.

"Wassup, bruh." He dapped me up before grabbing a cup to make him some coffee. He was one of the few people here I didn't have to code-switch with. He was from the Atlanta area, too, which I quickly picked up on when we first met. It was nice to have someone here that's familiar with where I'm from.

"You straight?" he asked.

I shrugged and nodded a little. "As straight as I can be. I worked from home for a few days so I could be home with my wife." After talking to Johnny about why I needed to stay home, I'm sure some people had heard about what happened. Thankfully, no one brought it up or showed fake sympathy.

Bernard exhaled. "How is she doing?"

"She's okay. I'm a little worried about her, but I think it's because she's by herself. I ain't really wanna leave her."

"I feel you. My wife had a hard time when we had our miscarriage, too."

I frowned slightly. "Word?"

He nodded. "Yeah. It happens to more people than you'd ever know or imagine." He paused for a second studying my face and body language. "How are you feeling, though?"

I shook my head not knowing how to respond. Every time someone asked me that question, I couldn't help but feel like I had no right to feel any type of way. Was I sad? Of course. Was I scared, too? Absolutely. Confused? Definitely. But how do I express that without feeling like it was unfair for me to feel like that at all? I sniffed trying to keep the tears at bay. I'd been emotional throughout all of this but did my best to hide it from Kyrah. I didn't want to make things worse for her.

"Honestly... I feel helpless," was all I could muster up to say.

"That's common, too, bro."

A sigh of relief escaped my lips as I listened to someone affirm my feelings. It was like God placed this dude right in my path just for this moment when I needed him the most.

He placed a hand on my shoulder. "I know how hard it is to watch your wife go through something traumatic. It's heartbreaking, honestly. But you're doing exactly what she needs." A brow raised as confusion spread across my face. "Just being here, being present, and loving her through it no matter how hard it is to watch her go through this. She appreciates it more than you know."

I blew out a breath and rubbed a hand down my face to wipe away the tears that managed to escape. I appreciated this conversation and his encouragement. But it did nothing but make me want to go back home and be with Kyrah. I just needed more time with her.

"I think I'ma go home early," I said. He removed his hand from my shoulder and nodded.

"That's a good idea, man. I'll tell Johnny I'll handle your files for the day." I held out my hand to dap him up.

"Thanks, man. I'll see you tomorrow."

"Bet."

I headed out of the breakroom and into my office to pack my things while simultaneously dialing the office phone for Johnny's office. After talking with him for a few minutes, he approved my request to leave early. Admittedly, I was feeling emotionally drained, and I just wanted to get home and hold my wife. I hadn't been at work that long, but I couldn't stay any longer. I had to get out of here.

The drive home seemed to take forever. It was lunch hour, so everyone was out grabbing food or going to the gym or whatever they chose to do. Kyrah and I hadn't talked much throughout the day. I figured she was probably asleep. I pulled up her number on the CarPlay screen and called her.

"Hey, baby," she answered sweetly.

I smiled in relief. "Hey, babygirl. I'm on the way home."

She chuckled, "What? Why are you coming home?"

"I just miss you... Wanted to come home to be with you."

"I miss you, too. Hurry home, then."

We hung up and suddenly the next ten minutes seemed to fly by. I pulled up to the front of our house not caring about any of my belongings in the car. I grabbed my phone and keys and headed inside the house after locking the car. Kyrah's eyes met mine when I opened the door. She was sitting on the couch, holding a book with her glasses on. She smiled. Her smile unlocked a mix of emotions. Tears streamed down my face unwarranted. I walked over to her slowly. She frowned as I got closer once she saw my face.

"Anthony, what's wrong?" She placed the book down and opened her arms welcoming me to come closer. I sat down and rested in her embrace. Usually, I'm holding her, but I need her right now. I couldn't keep these emotions inside anymore. I'm strong. But I guess I needed a release. She rubbed my back and I lay on her chest with silent tears falling. I inhaled and exhaled her gentle scent.

"It's okay, baby," she said softly. I sat up and looked at her. Her gaze was so tender and comforting.

"I'm sorry," I said chuckling a little. "I guess I'd been holding that in. Emotions got the best of me today."

She frowned and placed a hand on my cheek. Her thumb swiped a few tears away.

"Stop. Thank you for trusting me enough to do that... I know this has not been easy for you, too. But I'm here for you just like you've been here for me. We're going through this together. And we will be fine. That's what you keep telling me."

I smiled as I leaned in to kiss her soft lips. I sighed into, it restraining myself from taking it further. Her body was still healing, and her midwife recommended waiting at least two weeks before having sex. She groaned in frustration making me laugh.

"I know, baby. One more week," I said pulling away slightly.

She sighed and chuckled. "That's so long from now." She paused, then gasped after an idea popped into her brain. Her eyes grew big. "What about—?"

I shook my head and laughed. "Not that either. Trust me... I looked it up."

"UGH!" she said in frustration while laughing. "This week better go by fast." I leaned in and kissed her lips once more.

"It will, horn-ball," I reassured her.

She rolled her eyes, "Takes one to know one."

I chuckled before attacking her with kisses.

Chapter Eighteen

Things were finally starting to feel normal again. I'd had another appointment with my midwife confirming that everything looked good. She'd also given me some numbers of fertility specialists to contact in case we were interested in looking at our options in the event that we wouldn't be able to conceive. That was a reality I wasn't ready to accept. I refused to accept it. My heart wouldn't let me believe that even if a part of my brain had already come to terms with it.

I'd also avoided talking to Moriah because truthfully, I felt a little upset after she'd told me to have hope. I know it wasn't her fault, but deep down I felt like she'd sold me a dream full of false optimism and dreams. My story wasn't like hers. She had her rainbow baby. I'm still waiting for mine.

I sighed as I opened my laptop waiting for her to join the session. My phone vibrated alerting me that Anthony texted me. It always amazed me how he could still send butterflies to my stomach just like he did when we first met in college.

Hey, sweetheart. Just checking on you. I miss you. Put on something nice. We're going out tonight.

I smiled and quickly texted him back.

Hey, handsome. I miss you, too. I'll be ready.

My computer chirped letting me know that Moriah was signing on. Her face appeared on the screen, and she smiled warmly. I returned the smile, genuinely happy to see her.

"Hi, Kyrah," she greeted.

"Hey, Moriah."

"How are you doing, today? It's been a while since we last talked" she asked like she always does.

I blew out a long breath before responding. How was I doing, now? I couldn't put it into words. At the moment, all I could feel was excitement about going on a date with my husband. We needed this night out. A night of closeness. Intimacy. It's been a rough few months for us and I was very tired of dwelling on our tragedy.

"I think I'm okay, now..." I said with a little confidence.

She nodded. "You look a little hesitant, there."

I shrugged. "I honestly am."

"I'm curious to know why," she urged gently.

"Well," I started, contemplating my thoughts. They felt a little all over the place as I tried to put a name to my feelings. "I didn't expect to feel this peaceful after the second miscarriage. It was rough when it first happened... But... I think I expected it...? And that sounds horrible to say out loud." I facepalmed slightly. A deep sigh left my chest. "I'm just trying to accept what's happened to me."

She listened attentively before responding. The silence lingered for a while which was surprisingly nice. It gave me time to process what was going on in my brain.

"Kyrah, I think I know what could help you cope with your feelings and your thoughts," she countered. I nodded waiting for her to continue. "You should share your story."

I twisted my lips and frowned, unsure of what she meant. On top of that, I wasn't sure if I really wanted to relive these events. She chuckled as she noted the confusion on my face.

"What I mean is," she continued, "talking about it may be a good way to better understand your own experience. On top of that, it could be helpful to someone else who has gone through something similar. Miscarriages are far more common than most people think. Some women have them without even knowing if it happens within the first five weeks. It just feels like a regular period."

My eyebrows raised in shock. I couldn't imagine that. But ever since it's happened to me, I have done some research and have learned just how common this is. It's hard to talk about, so a lot of people don't share it which is understandable.

"It's just something to think about... Maybe a book... a blog... a vlog...? Something to share your story and your journey. I don't know why—and I have to take my counselor hat off for a moment—but I feel that God is going to use your story for something. To help someone else. Your voice is needed. Someone needs to hear this and see how you are coming out on the other side of it."

I wish I could hug her. I have done what I can to stay connected to God... And it has not been easy at all. Doubtful thoughts plagued my mind so often, but I'd try to counter those thoughts by thinking about my mom and Moriah. They both experienced loss and here they are. I can be like that.

"Again, no pressure," she smiled. "It's just a suggestion. Promise me you'll think about it, pray about it."

I nodded and returned the smile. "For sure."

***

I stood in my closet searching for the perfect outfit. I wanted to keep it simple. Simple has been my style lately. I know I'm supposed to be ready by the time Anthony gets here, but he's already on the way and apart from showering, brushing my teeth, and putting on some very light makeup, I am nowhere near ready. I sighed as I skimmed through all my dresses with my towel wrapped around my body. I heard the front door shut and his heavy footsteps coming up the stairs. I rolled my eyes knowing I was about to hear an earful. To my surprise, a chuckle came from him as he got closer.

"Wear the black one," he said as he walked in the closet wrapping his arms around my waist. His lips met my neck and I smiled. I pulled the black dress down and held it up against my body.

"I hope this still fits. I gotta lose some weight," I joked. He spun me around and smacked me on the butt before lightly grabbing as much as he could.

"Now you know I'm not willing to let this go," he said seriously, yet amused still holding my butt.

I smirked and giggled, "Unhand me, sir." He laughed as he removed his embrace to find himself something to wear. I watched as he walked out to go take a quick shower. As I walked back into the room, I caught a glimpse of myself in our full-body mirror. I let my towel drop and I slipped the dress up my body. My hands smoothed the dress over my hips, and I smiled. For the first time in a while, I felt beautiful. I felt peaceful. And I was more than ready to spend this much-needed time with Anthony.

For my hair, I settle for a messy bun with a few loose strands here and there. One last look in the mirror as I put on some diamond studs and clear lip gloss, and I decided that I was almost ready. Anthony walked over to me as I sat down to put on my heels and gently grabbed them from me. I giggled as I watched him kneel to put them on for me.

"I can put my own shoes on," I said amused as I watched him fasten my heels. He slowly caressed my calf and smirked as he looked into my eyes, biting his bottom lip slightly. His gaze lingered.

"I know you can..." he responded lowly still softly caressing my leg. My breath caught as I watched the look in his eyes change. Heat radiated off my body as we stared at each other.

"Anthony..." His name left my mouth, barely audible.

"I know... We have to go..." He slowly stood up and held out his hand to help me stand up. He snaked one arm around my waist and slowly leaned down to kiss me. The kiss was just to show me what was waiting for me when we got back home. And to be honest, I would've been okay with missing out and staying home so this man could have his way with me.

"You know what seeing you in heels does to me," he said lowly trying to restrain himself. I wish he wouldn't. I shook my head.

"My brain is a little foggy with you so close to me like this."

He chuckled. "I would hate for all this time spent on getting ready to go to waste... But I'm really struggling right now. You have no idea how much I want to take this dress off you." His hand slowly traveled down my back stopping at my butt.

I bit my bottom lip softly. "I think I do."

His eyes searched mine trying to analyze what was going on in my brain. If he could read it, he'd be pleasantly surprised at what he found.

We were on the same page. We both wanted the same thing. Right now. A pained look spread across his face giving me insight into the internal battle he was having.

"Kyrah... Whatever you want... Just tell me", he said roughly. I could tell he was trying not to lose his composure by how his hands were traveling up and down my back. The tone of his voice, the look in his eyes. The feel of his hands on my back was almost enough to make me melt in the palm of his hands. My body was on fire.

I sighed with furrowed eyebrows in sexual frustration. "I want you. Now," I breathily admitted.

He frowned as a low grunt escaped his throat. Without another word, he pulled down the straps of my dress as he kissed me passionately, claiming my lips like only he could. My hands found the bottom of this shirt, unbuttoning it to take it off him. Our lips remained connected as each layer of clothing was peeled off our bodies. My hands carved his toned abs and chest once his shirt was opened. He grunted lowly in response to my touch. Immediate moans and soft whimpers escaped my lips just from feeling his hands on my yearning skin. It's been weeks since I felt the closeness and the touch of my husband. Something my heart and body were craving after the series of pain we endured. We both needed this. We needed something to make us feel like *us* again.

Many sounds filled our room as we connected with one another. Anthony touched me and made love to me as if he'd never get the chance to again. And I enjoyed every second of it. His eyes locked onto mine surfacing a slew of emotions. Happiness, peace, love, and longing.

"I love you so much," he said with passion dripping from every word with his forehead resting on mine, our lips touching.

I sighed from the earth-shattering pleasure. "I love you, too."

We had time to go out whenever we wanted to, but I couldn't pass up this moment. Our bodies were magnetic and there was nothing that could keep us away from one another. There was no fighting the feeling and heat that was flowing through my blood for this man. He made me forget everything. All that matters is him. Us. And I love him for it.

Chapter Nineteen

overcomer...

The next week flew by. Anthony and I finally decided to tell our families and friends about the last pregnancy. It was a little hard to do for me, but I didn't want to keep it from them. It wasn't a secret in any way. I just didn't want to relive it. But as expected, everyone offered their support and love, which was all we needed. Once we told Tamra and Sean, they made immediate plans to visit us. They flew in Saturday morning with plans to stay for the week. It was so good to see them again. Raynah and Tommy couldn't come because they couldn't get off work, which I understood.

The boys went out to get us food for the night while Tamra and I were sitting on the couch talking with the TV playing in the background.

"Kyrah, I appreciate you guys letting us crash here again," she said sincerely.

I smiled, "Of course. You know y'all are always welcome here. We love having you."

She smiled as she studied me for a second. A sigh left her lips as if she was contemplating her next words.

"How are you?"

I shrugged. "I'm good," I responded quickly.

"'Good?'"

I hesitantly nodded, unsure of how to respond.

"'Good' is a state of being, my sweet friend... How are you feeling?"

Stunned. One thing about Tamra, she was never afraid of speaking her mind and telling the truth. It's one of the qualities that made me drawn to her as a friend. I looked at her and blinked a few times before forming an answer.

"I... feel indifferent." I didn't have any other words. Some days I was great, other days, not so much. And then there were days like today where I just didn't really feel. I just didn't want to think about it. I disassociated.

She smiled slightly and nodded. "I don't want to bring anything up. I know you and Anthony have been coping and dealing with everything. But I just wanted to ask you because sometimes we have this habit of holding in our true feelings by trying to tough it out. I don't want that for you. I was here when you first found out about the first pregnancy. And I wish I could've been here for you throughout all of it. But look at you... You are so strong, and not that you have to be, but here you are coming out on the other side of everything." She wiped a tear that escaped away from her cheek. "But I just want you to know that however you are feeling is okay. Indifferent is okay."

I looked at her with tears in my eyes. Tamra was always so vocal about making sure I was okay. She's always looked out for me ever since I met her in college. I met her before I met Raynah freshman year since we'd moved in on the same day. The first thing she told me was "We're gonna be great friends. From here on out, I got your back." And she had absolutely kept her word since then. How could I not appreciate her for it?

I didn't respond. Instead, I just leaned over and pulled her in for a hug. No words would come to me. It felt like that was just a moment where I needed to listen and allow myself to feel my emotions. While I'd been grieving the loss of our babies, I had a hard time understanding exactly what I was feeling. Tamra had no idea how much she'd just helped me. We pulled away from the embrace and took a deep breath simultaneously.

"Thanks, Tam," I said with a cracked voice. She wiped the tears from my face and smiled.

"Any time, girl."

I sighed. "My therapist, Moriah, told me that I should share my story. Write a blog or something." I chuckled at the thought. I'd considered her suggestion, but I couldn't realistically picture myself doing that. Who would actually be interested in hearing what I have to say? How could I inspire people by telling this sad story? Tamra perked up when I said those words. A big smile spread across her face. I eyed her curious to hear her response.

"I agree with her," she said enthusiastically.

I shook my head and exhaled. "I don't know, Tam—"

"Listen. There are so many people that have experienced this same thing, but don't talk about it."

"But what would I even talk about? What would I say? 'Hey! I had two miscarriages, but I'm doing just swell?'"

She rolled her eyes and chuckled. "Kyrah. I'm serious. You wanna know what people want to hear? If I was someone who went through this, I would want to hear someone's true feelings about it. Something that I could relate to. So many women walk around feeling like it's their fault, like it's something they did. [*I can understand that...*] They want to hear someone say they know how that feels. They also want to see someone who is working through it daily, still trusting God, still being loved by their spouse and loved ones... But also, the bad days when it's too hard to think about and they start questioning everything again. When they grieve the loss again, wishing they could've met their baby. Is that not you?" *Oh, she just read me for filth.*

I averted my eyes to my lap processing every single thing Tamra just said. She was right. And it was time I started listening. I shook my head and looked at her. Her face beamed.

"All I'm sayin' is... It seems like you're the chosen one to do this," she finished.

I chuckled. "I guess, Tam."

She smacked her teeth. "You are so damn stubborn, I swear."

"I tell her that every single day," I heard Anthony's voice say as he and Sean walked in with our food.

"That's your wife," Tamra said while laughing.

"Y'all leave my sis alone, nie," Sean said. I laughed and shook my head.

"Thank you, SEAN!" I responded. Anthony handed me my food and leaned down to kiss me sweetly.

"You know I love you. I know who I married," he said amused. I rolled my eyes.

"Yeah, I bet you do." He sat beside me still laughing.

We all ate our food, enjoying our fellowship together. I loved that we could all talk as if we didn't talk often. I felt incredibly blessed to have close coupled friends who have been here through the course of our relationship.

Around 11:00 pm, we decided to call it a night and head to bed. After putting away leftover food and cleaning up trash, Anthony and I headed upstairs to our room. As I was putting on my pajamas, Anthony sat on the bed and watched me. A smile grew on his face.

I chuckled. "What?"

He shook his head. "Nothin'. I just like lookin' at you."

"Creep."

He rolled his eyes. "A'ight. I'm going to bed."

I laughed and walked towards him to stand between his legs. He placed his hands on my hips, looking up at me with the purest love in his eyes. I leaned down and kissed him slowly. He grunted into the kiss before chuckling.

"Babygirl," he said, breaking the kiss a little.

"Hm?" I responded lowly.

"You been actin' like a rabbit, lately," he joked.

I smirked and shrugged. "We have a lot of catching up to do."

He laughed and smacked me on the butt. "You right about that." A squeal escaped my lips as he pulled me down on the bed, making me laugh.

Chapter Twenty

answer the call...

I sat in front of my laptop at our dining table, staring at the screen trying to figure out what exactly I was doing. At this point, everyone had been telling me I should listen to Moriah, and I was becoming convinced. I figured if I'd heard from more than two people, this was something I needed to be doing. But what exactly am I supposed to say?

Anthony walked over and handed me a cup of coffee before he sat down across from me in front of his own laptop. A sigh left my lips.

"Thanks," I said, exhausted from wrecking my brain with ideas.

"You're welcome...?" he responded concerned. "What's wrong?"

I shrugged. "I really don't know what to write. If I'm supposed to do this, why am I having such a hard time?"

He chewed his bottom lip before responding.

"You're overthinking it, baby." I stared at him waiting for him to continue because I definitely didn't agree with that statement. If anything, I couldn't think of anything at all. He chuckled reading my expression.

"Your whole life so far is a great story."

I frowned slightly. "What you mean?"

He sighed a little. "Think about it. You were a virgin when we met because you wanted to wait until marriage."

I laughed, "We both know how that ended."

He smirked. "Yes... but it's still something you can share. You can talk about our first go at our relationship and how God brought us back together, even throw that idiot Jesse in there."

"Anthony..." I said with an amused grin.

He laughed and held up his hand. "My bad. Anyway, talk about your depression and how you came out of that. But especially share your miscarriage stories. People need to hear this stuff, Kyrah."

I twisted my lips as I listened to him. I have been through a lot and have often joked about how someone could make some money off my life. Perhaps there was a testimony in here somewhere. Maybe someone could look at me and say, "Wow. That sounds like me." Suddenly, my brain birthed a few ideas to start.

"Okay, I think I have something."

He smiled. "Good. Now get to work."

I rolled my eyes. "You are not my daddy."

He scoffed. "Yeah, a'ight. That's not the same energy you had last night—"

"ANYWAY! I have work to do," I responded, suppressing a laugh. He laughed and resumed working on his laptop. I stared at my screen once more before my fingers started typing away.

Hi, there.

Welcome to the *Called to Overcome Blog.*

My name is Kyrah, and this is my first blog. I'm not exactly sure what I'll be writing about. So far, all I have is a name. But hopefully, you'll stick around long enough while I'll figure it out.

But to start, I guess I'll tell you a little bit about myself. I'm 25 and trying to figure out my life, to be honest. I'm married to the most handsome man in this entire world. He's what I consider my college sweetheart. It was a complicated situation at first, but we were so in love, we just couldn't stay away from each other, lol. But that's another story for another day. Perhaps you guys would like to hear that first?

You might be wondering why I'm writing this blog. Well, I'm wondering that, too. To be honest, I was told to do this a while ago, but I wasn't sure if I should. I honestly felt like I didn't really have anything to talk about. My life didn't seem that interesting to me. But my husband told me that I have a story that many people need to hear about. So, here we are. (:

Anyway, I think I've rambled enough for now. I think I'm going to start a series about my single-to-married journey. It is a pretty interesting one... Well, I guess that's it for now. I'll see you guys in the next one.

Bye for now!

Kyrah W.

I read over the words and surprisingly, I was proud of it. A smile grew on my face as I prepared myself to share it on a blogging website. There was no telling how or if anyone would actually read this, but I'm willing to try. Initially, the idea of putting myself out made me nervous. It felt too vulnerable. But I thought about how I would read other peoples' blogs from time to time, eager to learn more about what they had to say. Thinking about it made me excited to do this. I just hoped it was well received. It felt mediocre at best, but I know as time goes on, it'll get better.

I hit "submit" and exhaled deeply. There it was. Live on a public website for others to read.

"I did it." Anthony looked up from his computer and smiled. He held out his hand for me to place mine in.

"I'm proud of you."

"Thank you, baby. I'm proud of me, too."

Part Three

Chapter Twenty-One

THE PERFECT GIFT...

December 24th, 2023

Hey friends,

Welcome back to my blog. (:

It's Christmas time and I am so excited. Can you believe how fast this year has gone by? I know I can't. Wow.

Anyway, this is my favorite time of the year, like many other people. I always look forward to this time because of tradition. Anthony and I are still figuring out ours, well, mainly me. He just goes with the flow. But I am thankful that he gets excited about it with me. For us, we like to watch a Christmas movie every night leading up to

Christmas with Charlie Brown being the last one. He also makes us some of his famous hot chocolate on Christmas Eve. Mmm. As a matter of fact, he's going to make it soon and I absolutely cannot wait.

We also like to open one gift before we go to bed. This year, I have a very special gift for him. I hope he likes it. I put a lot of thought into it, lol.

What are some of your favorite holiday traditions? Share them below! I would love to read them. (:

See you all in the next one.

Merry Christmas!

Kyrah W.

Christmas time. My favorite holiday. There's something so cozy and comforting about this time of the year. Ever since Anthony went home with me in college during the holiday season, he has gone the extra mile to make it special.

I was wrapping the final, but most special gift to go under our Christmas tree while Anthony was in the kitchen making us some homemade hot chocolate. Soft Christmas music was playing in the background and because I'm extra, we were wearing matching pajamas. He walked over to me with two mugs full of chocolatey goodness just as I was placing the gift on the table.

"Here you go, sweetheart," he said, handing me mine before sitting on the couch beside me.

I smiled and snuggled close to him, "Thank you, babe." The warm mug felt good in my hands as I brought the it to my lips to sip it. "Mmm" fell from my lips.

He wrapped one arm around me, pulling me closer, and chuckled, "I guess that means it's good."

"Oh, 'good' is not even the word, baby." A sly smile formed on his lips before he leaned over to kiss me on the cheek.

"So, what are we gonna do tonight?" he asked as he sipped his own hot chocolate.

I pulled away slightly and scoffed as I glared at him. "I can't believe you're asking me that."

He laughed, "I'm sorry. I just need a memory refresher. We've watched movies every night leading up to tomorrow, wrapped the gifts, listened to music, had cookies, we're drinking hot chocolate... I'm stuck, babe."

I rolled my eyes and laughed. "We gotta watch Charlie Brown's Christmas and open one gift before bed."

He nodded. "Right, right. I'm sorry." He pulled me back to him and kissed me.

"Mhm." He deepened the kiss making me smirk. "Sex on the couch isn't a part of the tradition."

"I think we can make it a part of it," he responded before leaning down to kiss my neck. A giggle filled my throat from the ticklish feeling of his soft lips on my neck.

"What about our hot chocolate?" I asked.

"We can warm it up. I'll make it quick." He placed his mug on the table beside him before doing the same with mine. I climbed onto his lap and reconnected our lips. He firmly held my hips as he moved his lips back to my neck.

"I guess we can make this a part of our tradition," I joked followed by a slight moan. His hand traveled up my shirt as he unhooked my bra. Every time he touched me, a warming sensation took over my body.

"Good," he said lowly. "Consider this your first gift." I giggled as he laid me back on the couch.

***

30 minutes later

We both sat on the couch disheveled, breathing heavily. Our eyes met before laughter filled the living room.

"Jesus," I said, still catching my breath.

He chuckled deeply as he stood up to put his underwear and pants back on.

"Merry Christmas," he joked.

I rolled my eyes, "Very funny."

I stood up and headed towards the guest bathroom to clean myself up. Once I finished, I put my clothes back on and joined Anthony on the couch where he already had Charlie Brown on the TV. I snuggled up to him and enjoyed the Christmas special. These were moments I always looked forward to. Creating my own traditions with my own family has always been a dream of mine. And despite our rough year with fertility, I was still very much looking forward to us starting our own family.

Once the special went off, we both had just enough energy to open one gift each. There was a very special gift that I wanted him to open first. It had been a very hard secret to keep to myself, but I hoped he would love it. After grabbing a gift from under the tree, he walked back towards me and handed it to me as he sat back down. I handed him his gift with a smile on my face.

"You go first," he said with a cute smile beaming on his face.

"Okay," I said chuckling. I carefully unwrapped the gift, my eyes widening once I was able to make out what it was. My very own Kindle.

"Oh, babe! I love it! It's so pretty." The feeling of holding the light contraption excited me. I was trying to get more into eBooks and had briefly mentioned an eReader of some sort. But I didn't even know if he heard me when I said it a while ago. This was the sweetest gesture. "Gift receiving" is not my love language at all, but knowing he was listening that closely to me made this so special.

"Thank you, baby," I said before leaning over to kiss him.

"You're welcome, babygirl."

"Okay, now, your turn."

He nodded before turning his attention to his gift. He slowly unwrapped completely oblivious to what it was. It was a small gift, but it was special. As soon as he unwrapped it completely, he laughed in disbelief. He held up the pregnancy test. I laughed. I don't know why we were laughing. Maybe because after all these months, we'd stopped trying and just started to enjoy each other. We just wanted to remember that we had one another. I'd finally taken Moriah's advice and started a small blog talking about my journey from singlehood to marriage and the losses. And I'll admit, it was a great distraction and reminded me of the many ways I'd already been blessed.

He looked at me lovingly leaning over to kiss me sweetly.

"You're really pregnant."

I nodded and smiled. "I am."

"When did you take a test?"

"A few days ago... I noticed I missed my period, so I thought I should take one just to be safe."

He smiled. "Are you nervous?"

I shrugged. "Not really. I think this is the one."

His smile brightened when he heard my words. I wanted him to know that I wasn't afraid of this anymore. We were going to be okay. This was going to be okay. Excitement filled my heart after I saw the positive plus sign on the test a few days ago. It was hard keeping it from him, but I figured it would make a nice gift. He had only brought up having a baby a few times in the past few months, but for the most part, we'd both been happy with our current situation.

"I love you," he said leaning towards me.

"I love you, too." Our lips met, creating the perfect ending to our perfect Christmas Eve.

***

One Week Later

"Well, Kyrah and Anthony, I know we haven't seen each other in a while, but I'm so happy to see you again," Sarah said with a warm smile.

I smiled back. "I'm happy to see you, too. I think this is the one."

She nodded with a gentle grin still plastered on her face.

"So, you're about ten weeks?"

I nodded my head a little unsure. "I think so."

"Well, let's check it out so we can make sure." After setting everything up, she prepared me for the vaginal ultrasound like last time. After removing my pants and underwear, I sat back down in the seat. My nerves were starting to get the best of me as she leaned the chair back to examine me. I closed my eyes and said a quick prayer to myself.

Anthony gently grabbed my hand and squeezed it. My eyes met his warm chocolate brown eyes.

Sarah turned off the light, making me turn my attention to the screen. I blew out a nervous breath. *Please, be there...* All of this was starting to feel familiar. Some small part of me didn't want to go through this again, but I knew I needed to face the music. So many thoughts drowned out Sarah's voice no matter how hard I tried to focus on what she was saying. Until I heard it. The sound. The sweetest sound.

"And there's little bean's heartbeat. It's a strong one, too."

My eyes filled with tears. I looked at Anthony and noticed the gorgeous smile on his face. I exhaled, letting the happy tears flow.

"Wow," Anthony said.

"I'm so happy for you guys. And I agree, Kyrah... I think this is the one, too." I wiped my face and chuckled. After about ten more minutes, she finished checking everything to make sure everything looked fine prior to sitting me back up. She handed me some tissue to clean myself off before putting my clothes back on.

"Okay, so you are ten weeks. Congratulations!"

"Thank you," responded with a smile.

"You will need to come see me again in about two weeks. This is technically considered a high-risk pregnancy for now because you have had two miscarriages back-to-back. So, we want to make sure this pregnancy goes smoothly," she continued.

I nodded, "Okay. Sounds good." She turned off the screen, turned the lights back on, and sat back down in her seat. I pulled my pants up and sat back down waiting for her to continue telling me everything I needed to do to take care of myself.

After all this time, I couldn't believe it. Hearing the baby's heartbeat made it feel so real. There was still a twinge of sadness from missing out on this special moment with the other two babies, but I believe in my heart that this baby will help heal those wounds in my heart.

Chapter Twenty-Two

August 19th, 2024

"Babygirl, our reservations will be ready in about thirty minutes. We need to head to the hotel," Anthony said walking into the room. Yes, I was taking forever to pack. This pregnant belly was not allowing me to move any faster.

I sighed. "I'm going as fast as I can."

He smirked, "What can I help with?"

My eyes landed on my shoes then down to my feet.

"Can you help me put my shoes on?" I asked with a light giggle.

He chuckled, "You know what happened last time I put your shoes on for you." He made his way over to me and knelt down to grab my sneakers.

A frown etched my forehead. "That was your fault. You get turned on so easily."

He shrugged, "I have no shame."

I laughed and shook my head. My shoes were on. My bags were packed. My energy was low. I couldn't wait to get to our destination so I could rest.

We double-checked and made sure everything for our baby-moon/anniversary staycation was packed up and ready to go. Anthony surprised me with this local weekend trip as a way to relax before the baby came as well as one of my anniversary gifts. He told me he wanted to take me on an actual trip, but he didn't want to risk any complications because I was so far along in pregnancy. But he did manage to get us reservations at a beautiful hotel that had a spa service. I was so excited.

Thankfully we were able to beat traffic on the way downtown. My already swollen feet were happy about that. Anthony got us all checked into our room, and we hurried upstairs to our room so I could lie down for a little while.

"I'm sorry I couldn't take you on an actual trip for our anniversary," Anthony apologized for the millionth time. I shook my head.

"Babe, stop. This is absolutely perfect. Staycations are fun, too." I smiled and scooted over on the bed so he could sit with me. He sat down and wrapped one arm around me.

"Well, get some rest. We're going to dinner tonight. I'ma lay here and watch some TV."

I nodded and kissed his cheek before lying down and resting my eyes.

***

After a long nap, I felt refreshed. I laughed a little hearing Anthony still snoring. One thing that man was gonna do was snore loudly. I checked the time on my phone and saw that it was after 5 pm.

"I can't believe I slept that long. Sheesh." I tapped Anthony to wake him up so we could start getting ready. He yawned and stretched before flipping over to look at me.

"I don't even remember falling asleep," he sneered.

A smirk grew on my lips. "I bet you don't."

We both slowly but surely made our way out of bed and started preparing for dinner. Instead of going out, we just went to grab dinner in the downstairs restaurant. My eyes scanned the place.

"Babe, how much did you spend to get us a room here?" I asked curiously. He laughed deeply.

"You so damn nosy."

I rolled my eyes, "I'm just asking. This place looks expensive."

He bit his bottom lip before bringing his drink to his lips. "Don't worry about it, sweetheart."

I shuddered in reaction to him calling me that. I don't know what it was about that pet name, but it drove me crazy... in a good way. On top of that, my hormones have been a little high so there was a guarantee that we would be having some grown time after dinner.

He smirked, "You good?"

I nodded and looked down at my food, suddenly losing my appetite. One of the downsides to pregnancy was the appetite thing. Although I'd heard about that plenty of times before, I quickly learned that I was not prepared for it at all. But overall, this pregnancy has been nothing short of amazing. And Anthony has been wonderful. Every day, he showed me just how much he loved me and how excited he was to be starting this family with me.

"I lost my appetite," I said slightly embarrassed.

Anthony chuckled and nodded, finishing the last bite of his food.

"I'll eat it later," he said while rubbing his stomach. I chuckled.

"Greedy."

"I'ma eat you, too." He winked. My insides automatically melted.

"Let's go," I responded.

I woke the following morning to Anthony sitting on the edge of the bed with breakfast waiting for me. He smiled as I opened my eyes.

"Good morning, beautiful. Happy early anniversary. I ordered us some breakfast."

I smiled and slowly sat up.

"Happy early anniversary, baby." The baby started moving around making me chuckle a bit. I reached for Anthony's hand, placing it where the baby was kicking me. But as soon as Anthony's hand touched my stomach, the baby stopped.

He smacked his lips. I laughed hysterically.

"I swear, that baby got beef wit' me," he said shaking his head.

"She's gonna love you."

He frowned, "She? How you know we not havin' a 'he'?"

I rolled my eyes as I made my way to sit beside him. Lately, we've been having this playful disagreement about the gender of our baby. We made the decision early on to wait until we had the baby to learn the gender. Mainly because we just wanted to enjoy knowing that we were having a baby no matter what. This was a great decision for us.

"Anthony, I told you. I just know."

He smacked his teeth as he scooped up a spoonful of grits.

"Yeah, a'ight. You keep tellin' yourself that."

"And will." I retorted before taking a bite of bacon.

We ate our food while talking with the TV playing in the background. He told me that I needed to get ready since we'd be celebrating all day starting with a relaxing massage at the spa downstairs, followed by a mani/pedi for two, some shopping at the shops nearby, and a nice relaxing dinner on the rooftop jazz area.

"Wow, you really planned the day out," I said as I finished up my food.

He nodded, "I really want to make this special for you since we'll be having a baby soon."

I smiled and leaned over to kiss him softly on the lips.

"You're amazing," I said.

"Not as amazing as you." He pecked my lips. "Now come on. Let's get ready. Our massages start in two hours." I nodded and headed to the bathroom for a quick, but much-needed shower.

The massage was amazing. And the mani/pedi was so relaxing. I was very appreciative of the spa staff that took special care of me. At first, I was nervous because I didn't want to go into early labor, but they knew exactly what they were doing. And I also knew Anthony had already made sure of it.

As I was putting my earrings on for dinner, Anthony came behind me and wrapped his arms around me as much as he could. He placed his arms on my stomach.

"You look breathtaking," he said softly in my ear.

I smirked, "You said that at our wedding."

His lips met the back of my neck. "I meant it then, and I mean it now."

I turned my body around and looked up in his eyes.

"You tryna turn me on? Because it's working."

He chuckled, "And you call me a hornball."

I rolled my eyes and laughed, "Whatever. I'm ready." He nodded and gently grabbed one of my hands to lead me out of the bathroom. We both grabbed everything we needed and headed out the door.

The rooftop restaurant was absolutely beautiful. I truly appreciated how Anthony always gave me a city view whenever he could. I looked to the side and stared at all the lights in the sky.

"This is absolutely gorgeous," I complimented.

He smiled his beautiful smile. "I'm glad you like it. Ready for your gift?"

My eyes grew big as I dug in my purse for his.

"Wait! Let me go first." He chuckled and nodded. I grabbed the gift out of my purse and handed it to him. He shook it a little before eyeing me skeptically.

"What is it?"

Playfully annoyed, I rolled my eyes. "Open it, silly."

He ripped open the gift wrap, his mouth dropping and his eyes growing big.

"Kyrah..." he said as he held his Galaxy watch that he'd been eyeing for a while.

I chuckled, "You like it?"

He nodded, "Absolutely. Thank you, baby. I can't wait to wear this work." My smile widened as he stared at it in amazement. I truly married a tech nerd. It doesn't take much to please Anthony. He is genuinely appreciative of anything I give him, so I try to give him the things that he truly wants.

"Okay, your turn," he said handing me my bag. He always seemed to outdo me with gifts. I took the bag and pulled the gift paper out of the bag to see what was at the bottom. My eyes widened at the sight.

"Anthony... What—"

"I noticed you were getting slightly frustrated with your computer," he stopped and chuckled. "So, I went and got you a new one that has more space so you can write. You seem to have fallen in love with writing and I want to invest in that, even if it's just a hobby."

The tears. I couldn't stop them. This man is always so sweet to me. He always pays attention. I have been frustrated with my computer because it was starting to move slower. There just wasn't enough space on it for the amount of writing I was doing. Plus, I still had old schoolwork on there that I had been procrastinating to delete, including the work from the master's program I decided not to finish. I shook my head and wiped the hormonal tears from my face.

"Thank you so much, baby. You truly are the best thing that's ever happened to me."

He smiled. "Happy anniversary, sweetheart."

I returned the smile, "Happy anniversary, baby." I took a deep breath and started scooting my chair back.

"What you doin'?" he asked, amused.

"Let's go. I'm ready for dessert."

His eyebrows raised as he quickly stood up to help me get up. "Oh, you ain't gotta tell me twice. Let's go."

Chapter
Twenty-Three

THE BEST EXPERIENCE...

1:40 a.m.

August 23rd, 2024

I woke up feeling like I was peeing on myself. A huge puddle in the bed, soaking our sheets. My initial thought was to panic because I had no idea what was happening for a split second. Then it dawned on me. I tapped Anthony and sat up slowly.

"Anthony, get up," I said waking myself up all the way.

"Hm?" he groggily responded. "What's going on?"

I sighed and cautiously stood up from the bed.

"My water broke. I'm going to clean up real quick."

"WHAT?!" he panicked. He jumped out the bed and grabbed random clothes to throw on. I stood there and watched him run around the room frantically. The laugh that was building up in my belly was hard not to let out. He looked at me as he was putting his shoes on and frowned.

"Kyrah, don't just stand there! We gotta go!"

I laughed hysterically. "Babe, calm down. First of all, you have your shorts on the wrong way. Second of all, you have two different shoes on. And third of all, we have time. My contractions haven't started, yet. Remember, Sarah told us that once the contractions start, we need to pay attention to how close together they are and how long they last."

He closed his eyes and exhaled before letting out a deep laugh.

"Sorry," he apologized still laughing.

I chuckled and shook my head. "Call Sarah and tell her my water broke. I'll be in the shower. Can you change the sheets?"

He nodded, "I gotcha, baby. Go get cleaned up. Let me know if they start." I nodded and smiled.

I waddled my way to the bathroom to clean myself off. As I was lathering my washcloth, I felt the strongest cramp in my belly.

"Woah!", I exclaimed. It lasted for what felt like thirty seconds. Was that a contraction? I shook my head and kept washing myself. About eight minutes later, another started up. Yep. Definitely a contraction. Sarah's instructions came back to my memory as I faced yet another contraction. "Take deep breaths, Kyrah". I closed my eyes and took slow deep breaths, fighting the urge to groan from the slight pain. However, I knew I needed to hurry up because it was only going to get worse from there. I stepped out of the shower and quickly dried myself off.

"Babe, they started!" I called out.

Anthony came rushing in and helped me finish drying off and putting some comfortable clothes on. He was calmer now. And as supportive as I needed him to be. Our hospital bags were waiting for us by the door so all we had to do was grab them and walk out the door. Contractions interrupted us a few times, but not enough to slow us down. Once we got in the car, the contractions picked up. Anthony made a quick call to Sarah.

"Hey, Sarah. We're on the way to the hospital. Her contractions are still spread apart... Okay... We'll see you there... Bye." He glanced over at me and smiled before grabbing my hand to kiss.

About three minutes later, we pulled into the parking lot of the hospital. Anthony grabbed all of our belongings and followed me inside. They quickly checked me in at the L&D wing and took us to our delivery room. I exhaled and felt the emotions flooding me. This is really happening. Our first baby.

I lay in the bed with my delivery gown on, soft music playing, and an air mist machine. Anthony stayed by my side the whole time, massaging my back through every contraction. Sarah met us at the hospital and stayed with us. She rubbed my hips to help me relax during the contractions. The pain was a lot, to say the least. Nothing like what I expected.

"You're doing good, babygirl," Anthony encouraged me. I exhaled slowly as the contraction passed.

"I can't believe I prayed for this child, and she treats me like this," I joked. Anthony laughed and placed his forehead on mine. He planted a sweet, slow kiss on my lips.

"Uhn-uhn. Back up. You're the reason I'm in pain," I joked again. He chuckled and kissed me on the forehead.

My smile was quickly replaced with a frown as another contraction started. Anthony pulled away and held my hand to soothe me.

"I feel like I have to poop," I whimpered from the pain.

"It's time," Sarah said. The two nurses who had been assisting her set everything up for me to push. They got the squat bar and the foot elevation support up for me to push in different positions. I looked at Anthony who was staring at me, slightly concerned.

"You ready?" he asked.

I smiled and nodded. "Let's have a baby."

"Alright, Kyrah. Next contraction, I want you to take a deep inhale and push on exhale, okay?" I nodded. She watched the monitor closely and noticed another one coming. "Okay, Kyrah. Get ready. Inhale." I followed her instructions. "Aaaaaand... exhale-push!"

I closed my eyes and pushed with all my might. Then I did it again on the next contraction. The entire time, I had a team of people cheering me on, and encouraging me, including Anthony who hadn't left my side the whole time we'd been here. He grabbed a towel and patted my forehead dry from the beads of sweat that formed. He kissed my forehead as I caught my breath. For the next forty-five minutes, I repeated the same steps.

"I see little bean's head," Sarah beamed. "I think one more push will do it." I closed my eyes feeling tired.

"Okay," I said exhausted. Sarah looked at me with concern.

"You can do this, Kyrah, okay? Your body was made for this. Just one more good push."

I smiled weakly, "Okay."

"Here it comes. Inhale." Everything seemed to move in slow motion. I took in a deep inhale. "Exhale. Push!" My face scrunched up as I pushed as hard as I could. I could feel the relief of the pressure from the baby. Then the sweetest noise filled my ears.

"Congratulations, guys. You have a baby girl," Sarah announced cheerfully.

I laughed through tears, "I told you we were having a girl." Anthony laughed and shook his head.

"You did it, baby," he said kissing me on the forehead. "I'm so proud of you."

Tears streamed down my cheeks as they placed our baby on my chest.

"She's beautiful," I said in tears.

"Just like you," Anthony said. I looked up to find him with a few tears on his cheeks. We were in awe of what our love made. The happiness that filled my heart couldn't be replicated in any way.

I smiled with tears in my eyes. "Look at what we made, baby."

Anthony chuckled, "I know. All that hard work paid off."

I laughed, "It sure did."

Chapter Twenty-Four

GOODBYE FOR NOW...

A few days have passed since I gave birth and being home with her has been nothing short of amazing. Anthony and I being parents felt so natural. I watched Anthony as he sat on the couch feeding our baby girl while I rested for a bit. She looked so peaceful in his arms. I couldn't be more thankful to God for answering our prayers and giving us our rainbow baby. She is beautiful beyond words. The joy I feel in my heart knowing that I have two people who love me unconditionally. What more could I ask for?

I sat at my computer writing my next blog post, ready to share this joyous gift with the world. Since I started sharing my story, I've heard from a few women who had experienced the same thing, and it warmed my heart to know that God could use my story to encourage others. He took my pain and used it to show others that they weren't alone and that miracles do happen.

Blogging has also opened the door for me to explore other forms of writing like storytelling. Who knew that this would be something I'd become passionate about? Well, I didn't see it coming, but I'm thankful to be doing it. A small smile formed on my lips as I wrote the words on my website:

God has blessed me tremendously. It feels like only yesterday I was the shy, timid, inexperienced girl in college who didn't know anything about love or herself; and she definitely didn't know anything about what God had in store for her. Sometimes I wish I could go back and give her the biggest hug. Everything that she went through was for this moment right here. All the people she met were for a reason, even the ones that hurt her.

She met some amazing friends who she can't imagine what it would be like to not have them in her life. And above all, she met the person who changed her life forever... the man who showed her what it feels like to love and be loved. At first, it may not seem like it, but he has always been that rock for her when she needed him... And he still is.

I have had my share of heartaches, depression, and uncertainty. But God has always been faithful enough to remind me that He is always with me. He has shown me that through examples and through people... Especially through Anthony. I sometimes have to pinch myself because I can't believe this is my life. But every morning I get to wake up to his handsome face and his loving kisses. And now I get to wake up to the most adorable face I've ever seen, who is a beautiful mixture of both of us.

I can never thank God enough... I can't wait to see what else He has in store for me.

Anyway, I have to go. My little family is waiting for me. Talk to you guys later!

Kyrah W.

...*Don't cry yet*...

Keep reading. (:

Epilogue I

DO IT AGAIN...

15 years later

"Can you believe our baby is getting ready for her first day of high school?" I said to Anthony while pouring him a cup of coffee. We stood in our rather spacious kitchen in our house in Augusta, Georgia. We moved back a few months after I had Karter. And it was a decision we were both happy with.

He shook his head. "I really can't. And Little man is getting ready to go to 7th grade. Where did the time go?"

I chuckled rubbing my pregnant belly. "You sure you wanna do this again? In our 40's?" I asked, slightly amused at us being 6 months pregnant again.

He smiled and walked towards me, wrapping his arms around my waist, and placing his large gentle hands on my belly.

"With you? Absolutely." He kissed me on the back of my neck.

I chuckled. "That's how we got into this mess in the first place." He let out a laugh as he backed away and smacked me on my butt.

"Can you guys please not be gross right now?" Karter said walking in the kitchen.

I giggled as I sat her plate of waffles and turkey bacon on the kitchen island.

"Thanks, Mom," she said sitting down. I winked at her and resumed making AJ's plate. Anthony walked over to sit beside Karter.

"Now how you think you got here?" he said sarcastically. "Anthony," I said in a warning tone with a slight hint of amusement.

"Ew, Dad! Gross!" Karter said. Anthony laughed before taking a sip of his coffee. I walked over to set his plate of turkey bacon, egg whites, and toast in front of him.

"Thank you, sweetheart. This plate looks almost as good as you."

I blushed and walked back to the stove.

"Where is your brother? He needs to come on. We have to go," I said exasperated. I had to be at my doctor's appointment before heading to a meeting with my book manager. Karter shrugged as she placed a forkful of waffles in her mouth.

"AJ!" I called out.

"Yes?", his puberty voice called out.

"Come on! We have to go!"

"Coming!" His footsteps carried all the way down the stairs, and he walked into the kitchen with his backpack on his back.

"Boy, what took you so long?" Anthony asked him. AJ smirked showing off the deep dimple in his right cheek and stroked his chin. We all stared at him waiting for him to answer. He looked around and smacked his teeth before rolling his eyes.

"Y'all don't see this?" he said pointing to his chin. He walked up to me, and I squinted my eyes to find the smallest chin hairs. I chuckled.

"Son, I don't see nothin', but I do smell you. Did you put deodorant on?" Anthony asked with a scrunched-up nose. AJ's eyes grew big as he sniffed his armpits.

"I'll be right back."

I shook my head as I watched him run off.

"Hurry, please! We need to go."

"Yes, ma'am!" he called back.

Karter stood up to place her plate and fork in the dishwasher.

"You know he has a girlfriend, right?" she said with a small smirk. I raised an eyebrow and looked at Anthony who quickly looked down at his plate.

"Anthony?"

"H-huh?" he stuttered with a mouth full of bacon.

"Did you know he has a girlfriend?" I asked calmly. It didn't upset me that he had a girlfriend. I was just annoyed at the fact that no one told me… and maybe these pregnancy hormones were heightening my emotions, too.

Anthony sighed as his eyes met mine. "Yeah, he told me. But thanks to Karter, I didn't get a chance to tell you."

Karter snickered and mouthed "sorry" before sipping her orange juice. I let out a deep breath and laughed a bit.

"I guess he'll tell me when he's ready." Both Anthony and Karter stopped in their tracks and looked at me skeptically. My eyes shifted between them confused. "What?" I asked. Anthony stood up and walked towards me. He lightly touched my forehead with the back of his hand. Karter walked over to me concerned.

"Mom, are you okay?" she asked. I frowned and shook my head.

"What are you two on about? And where the hell is AJ? —AJ!!!!!!!" They looked at each other and laughed.

"She's good," they said simultaneously.

"I'm coming, dang!" AJ responded.

He appeared in the kitchen with an annoyed expression. Anthony walked up to him and smacked him on the back of the head. "Ouch!" came from his lips making Karter snicker. My eyes met hers and she quickly stopped.

"Watch how you talk to my wife," Anthony said sternly. I shook my head and handed AJ his plate.

"You better eat fast because we have to go," I said walking away to put dishes in the dishwasher.

"Yes ma'am," he mumbled while rubbing the back of his head with his free hand.

I left everyone in the kitchen to finish getting ready. Anthony followed behind me and shut our bedroom door behind us. I hectically searched for my mascara and lip gloss to put on for this meeting. An exasperated sigh left my lips as I rushed to finish getting ready. Anthony started buttoning up his shirt and stared at me with love like he always does.

"Can I help you?" I asked with a shy smile. He smirked. After tucking his shirt in his pants, he walked towards me and kissed me on the forehead.

"Anthony, I am too damn old to be pregnant," I said chuckling.

When we found out about the third one, it was a complete shock. I was prepared for menopause to hit. All the symptoms felt like it. But my doctor took some blood work at my appointment and confirmed that I was carrying another little one. Because I'm older, I'm considered high risk which means I'm seeing my midwife and doctor a lot more than I did with the other two.

Anthony chuckled and wrapped his arms around me pulling me in for a sweet embrace.

"God thinks otherwise, babygirl."

I looked up at him with a small smile, admiring how handsome he looked. He'd cut his locs when we moved back to Augusta and has been rocking a faded, low-cut curly afro since then. Still fine as ever.

"You still call me that after all these years."

"You wanna know why?" I twisted my lips and nodded curiously.

I've always loved it when he called me that. Admittedly, I assumed he would stop once we had Karter because I figured he would be calling her that. And I didn't mind one bit. We'd been waiting and praying for our baby girl to come.

"I call you that because the first time I did in college, I paid attention to your reaction."

He moved a strand of hair from my face and tucked it behind my ear. His warm hand stayed on my cheek as his beautiful brown eyes looked deep into my eyes, making me fall in love with him even more.

"I wasn't sure what I would call you at first. But the first time I called you 'babygirl', you blushed. It was so cute. And I've wanted to make you blush every day ever since."

I bit my lip and smiled. "You're so cheesy."

He chuckled. "You love it, sweetheart."

I squinted my eyes. "What about that pet name?"

He raised an eyebrow and leaned down to kiss me on the neck before bringing his lips to my ear. My insides twisted, and it was *not* the baby moving.

"I call you that because I see how it turns you on." I sighed. My head involuntarily tilted allowing him access to my neck.

"Anthony, I have to go... and so do you."

He grunted. "I can't resist you, especially when you're carrying my seed." I giggle-moaned and gripped his still very toned arms. He brought his lips to mine, and we kissed passionately. The baby started moving around in my stomach making both of us laugh.

"We're ready, mom! I don't wanna be late!" Karter said from the other side of our door. I broke the kiss and sighed.

"Okay, honey. Give me one second." Anthony kissed me on the forehead and smiled.

"Let's get out of here. We'll finish this later."

I grinned and nodded.

***

"Kyrah, this book is amazing. It's going to do numbers," my book manager, Jeanie said. She shook her head in amazement as she flipped through the pages.

We'd finally received our proof copies to make sure everything was in place and exactly how I wanted it. The cover was amazing. I ran my hand over my personal proof copy and smiled.

"You think so?" I asked anxiously.

Writing the blog made me want to branch out with my writing. I fell in love with it. Moriah was right. I had so many stories that needed to be told. I still blog here and there, but my website now takes care of itself while I spend my time writing books. I'm still an indie author, but I have been consistently writing and self-publishing my books. And truthfully, I have been enjoying it more than I've ever enjoyed anything else. It fulfills me.

Jeanie smiled and nodded. "Girl, yes. This book is definitely giving 'Bestseller'."

I chuckled. "Anthony said the same thing."

She smirked and shrugged. "Your husband knows what he's talking about, girl."

My eyes rolled playfully. "Please, do not make his head bigger than what it is." We shared a laugh before our drink orders and pastries were delivered to our table.

"Okay, now let's talk release date. What are we thinking?" she asked pulling out a pen to write some notes down. "I have been looking at some places for us to do book signings."

I twisted my lips and tilted my head, thinking of a perfect date. The issue is there isn't one. I just know I wanted to do it before I had this baby.

"The sooner the better. I don't want to be promoting this book in the hospital. I'm six months so we have time. But we need to do it soon."

She nodded. "I agree. Okay, I will come up with some dates and we'll confirm either over the phone or via email."

"Okay. Sounds good."

She exhaled and stared at the book. "I can't get over this. This yellow cover with all the different art... The layers. It's beautiful Kyrah. And the story is spicy, which is very popular."

I smiled. "Thank you. '**See Me...**' is definitely outside of my comfort zone. But I love that I'm more comfortable with this topic of sex," I looked down at my stomach and pointed, "clearly." We laughed and she shook her head.

"Well, I know this one will have the readers sweating and falling in love with **Tre'Von**. It's going to be a hit."

"Thanks, Jeanie," I said with a genuine grin. I was ecstatic to share this story with the world. I just hoped it would be received well...

***

I pulled into our driveway with Karter and AJ in the car with me. Anthony told us to be ready to go out for a nice family dinner. Stress automatically filled my entire body at the thought of having to find something to wear. This pregnancy already hasn't been that easy. And as if that wasn't enough, one major issue I've had is finding clothes that fit. Anthony offered to buy me more, but I just didn't see a point in buying new clothes only to wear them for a few months. "I just want you to be comfortable, baby," was his favorite line whenever we had this conversation.

The three of us hurried out of the car and into the house to start getting ready so the man of the house wouldn't come home rushing us.

"Guys, no lollygagging. We need to be ready by the time your dad gets here."

"Got it, Mom," AJ said.

"Yes ma'am," Karter added. We all went our separate ways to prepare for dinner. As I walked into our room, I saw a pleasant surprise lying on my bed. A chuckle escaped my lips as I walked closer and saw a note lying beside it. I sat down on the bed to read, shaking my head in amusement at the words on the paper.

> **Hey sweetheart,**
>
> **I know you didn't want a new outfit, but I saw this and had to get it for you. I picked it up and dropped it off during my lunch break, lol. Anyway, put this on. You'll look very sexy in it. (; Can't wait to take it off you. See you soon.**
>
> **And y'all hurry up and get ready, please.**
>
> **~Anthony**

I rolled my eyes at the last part and laughed.

"That man is something else," I said to myself. At least now I didn't have to worry about finding something to wear. He'd bought me a beautiful black jumpsuit that made an 'X' across my back and showed a little cleavage. He also bought me a new pair of sandals to match. After all these years together, he's still doing things like this to make me smile.

I finally decided to stop wasting time and head to the bathroom to freshen up. I pulled my hair up into a high puff and touched up my mascara and lip gloss. Just as I was pulling the straps of the jumpsuit up on my shoulders, Anthony walked into the room.

"Babygirl," he called out.

"I'm in the bathroom," I called back. He walked in, his eyes widening instantly.

"Oh yeah... Let's just stay here. I'm ready to take that off you," he said walking towards me. I laughed and lightly pushed him away.

"I don't think so. I had to work to get this thing over this big ole belly."

He laughed quietly, "You look beautiful, baby."

I smiled, "Thank you.

We all headed out for a nice family dinner. Karter told us all about school and how she was planning to try out for the cheer squad. Anthony wasn't too keen on the idea, but he supported her, nonetheless. We always encourage our kids to try new things at least once. AJ told us more about his girlfriend. I asked him when he planned to introduce her to us and of course, with his smart mouth, his answer was "No time soon". My children are amazing. And now that we are having a third one in a few months, I feel confident and excited that they will be great examples for their little brother.

Epilogue II

LAST BABYMOON...

"Kyrah, only you would want to plan a babymoon at the last minute," Anthony said jokingly packing an overnight bag. I had the bright idea of going to Atlanta for two nights as a mini babymoon before I gave birth to our last baby.

I scoffed and rolled my eyes. "You know what? I'll go by myself since you wanna act like that."

He laughed, "Chill out. I'm just sayin'."

"Mmhm." I placed one last thing in the bag and zipped it up. This was a much-needed getaway. With my delivery date quickly approaching, I needed to be as relaxed as possible. On top of that, Anthony suggested I push the release date of my book back because he could see I was slightly stressed about it. I didn't agree with him at first, but I'm glad I listened to him. Jeanie also realized that it was a good idea and reminded me that my health and the baby were more important.

"I'm all packed up and ready to go," I said sitting down for a second.

"A'ight, gimme a second."

After waiting for Anthony for a few more minutes, we headed out of our room to get the kids so we could drop them off at Kyrie's house. They wanted to go spend the weekend with their cousins which works out perfectly for us.

"Let's go, y'all! Anthony called out.

"Coming!" Karter yelled out. She came out of her room with an overnight back and her cell phone. AJ practically ran out of his room with a backpack probably stuffed with random clothes.

"Do you guys have everything?" I asked.

"Yes ma'am," Karter responded.

AJ paused and thought about his answer. "Uh... I think so..." he responded unsure. I sighed while facepalming.

"Let's go over the list: Two pairs of clothes and PJs?" He nodded.

"At least three pairs of underwear?" Nodded again. "Deodorant? Toothbrush?" He nodded once more. "Phone and charger?" He snapped and shook his head.

"Forgot my charger. I'll be right back" I chuckled and shook my head in response. AJ was quite a character, but he always made me laugh. His humor was definitely his dad's on steroids. Anthony came back to the hallways where Karter and I were waiting for AJ.

"Y'all good?" he asked with impatience in his tone.

"Waiting for your son. He forgot his charger." Anthony's brows rose and he took off back down the hallway to our room.

"Where are you going??" I asked.

"Forgot my charger, too!" He called back.

I shook my head and looked at Karter. She shook her head while laughing quietly.

"What would men do without women?" I joked. "Let's go wait for them in the car."

***

I lay in the warm hotel bed snuggled up with Anthony. He rubbed my back, soothing me. I could go to sleep any moment. I exhaled softly, snuggling closer to him.

"I am so ready to have this baby," I expressed tiredly.

He chuckled, "I can tell. You look miserable most days."

A small laugh left my throat. "That's because I am. Being pregnant in your 40s is crazy work. My body is upset with me."

He inhaled deeply. "I think you should give your body more credit."

"What you mean?"

It was silent for a moment. "Your body has been through a lot. I know it's a little more taxing because we're in our 40s, but being able to carry a healthy baby at this age is a miracle and a blessing. And with your body going through so much in the past, I think it deserves some praise for all its hard work."

I sat up a little to find him looking at me with a smirk.

"Oh, you mean that kind of praise," I said catching his drift.

"Baby, what took you so long," he joked. I sat up with a smirk matching his and pulled my shirt over my head.

"Don't send me into labor with all this praise."

He sat up and kissed me slowly, sensually, arousing me completely.

"No promises," he said with his lips still on mine.

Epilogue III

New Journey

One month later

I stood backstage feeling every nerve in my body. My eyes closed as I blew out deep, slow breaths. Where are they?

"You ready, Kyrah?" Jeanie asked, touching my shoulder gently.

I shook my head, "I—" Before I could respond, my eyes met my favorite pair of brown eyes. Everything seemed to slow down. In his arms was our newborn baby boy, Aaron with Karter and AJ walking behind him. A grin slowly spread across my face as they approached me. Anthony stood in front of me, with a proud look on his face.

"Hey," he said lowly.

"Hi." I felt like I could finally breathe.

Many people came from across state lines just to come hear me speak about my new book. ***See Me…*** was a huge success which really surprised me. I never even dreamed of being a bestseller. I just write because I enjoy it so much. But knowing that so many people took the time to give this book a chance and truly enjoyed it warms my heart. And here I am standing backstage with my family waiting to be introduced as a guest to be interviewed.

"You ready?" Anthony asked. I walked closer to him, leaning in slowly for our lips to touch. Everything about this man inspired me. The sweet nature of Tre'Von from my book reminds me so much of my sweet husband. So caring. So gentle. His constant support is what keeps me going. He pushes me when I am unsure about myself. This is a love beyond my wildest dreams. And we have created three beautiful children from it. I'm blessed to have spent the last twenty years with him, and I sincerely pray that we get to have many more.

Our lips parted and I bit my bottom lip, smiling.

"I am now," I responded softly. Jeanie walked up to me with an eager expression.

"They're about to call you, Kyrah." I smiled and nodded.

"Good luck, Mom," Karter said with a smile.

"We're proud of you," AJ said. I chewed my bottom lip fighting back tears.

"I have all the blessings I need right here. I love you guys," I said backing away towards the entrance of the stage. My eyes met Anthony's and he mouthed "I love you" with a proud grin.

I blew a kiss before turning around waiting for them to call my name.

"It is my greatest honor and pleasure to introduce our next guest. This woman has written one of the greatest books to ever hit a bookshelf. Beyond that, she is the sweetest soul. Please stand to your feet and join me in welcoming the phenomenal author, Mrs. Kyrah Wright!" The host announced. I exhaled, silently thanking God for this incredible opportunity. A genuine smile formed on my lips as my feet started moving towards the stage. Loud cheers roared through the room as I walked out, looking around and waving.

I met the host in the middle of the stage and gave her a big hug. She greeted me and welcomed me to take a seat.

"Wow," I said taking it all in. She chuckled and nodded.

"Yes, girl. This is all for you. How does this feel?" I shook my head, not exactly sure how to describe the feeling.

"It's surreal, to say the least. If you would've asked me if I saw this in my future when I was 18, the answer would've been 'hell no'." Everyone laughed for a few seconds.

"Kyrah, I gotta say, we all love your book. '***See Me...***' is such a beautiful friends-to-lovers trope. And that Tre'Von—" someone from the crowd whistled interrupting her. I laughed a little. "He is a beautiful character. Is he inspired by someone?"

I nodded and blushed a little. "Yes. My husband."

"Aww" came flooded through the room. The smile on my face couldn't be contained. Any chance I had to talk about Anthony, I was taking it. I facepalmed not from embarrassment, but from knowing he was backstage completely feeling himself.

The rest of the interview was amazing. It felt natural. She asked wonderful questions that made me think and continuously complimented my writing style. This gave me confidence that I could really do this. It felt exciting. And now I can't wait to keep writing more stories for everyone to read.

"Well, one more thing, Mrs. Kyrah... Will there be another one in the future?" she asked. Everyone waited for my answer, and I looked around with a satisfied expression.

"Absolutely."

Everyone cheered and stood up, making me smile with pride.

"Let's give it up for Kyrah Wright one more time, ladies and gen-tlemen!" I stood up to hug the host one more time. I turned my head to look backstage, seeing my beautiful family cheering me on. This was a moment for all of us, a moment I wanted to share with them, too. I motioned for them to come stand with me. As they made their way out on stage, "Aww" flooded through the room. They stood with me, making this moment perfect. Anthony looked at me, still holding Aaron, and smiled.

"I'm proud of you," he said.

"Thank you, baby. I love you."

"I love you, more." He leaned down and kissed me tenderly, sealing the perfection of this moment... this new journey.

The End

Letter from the Author

Wow. I can't believe this series is over... I often reflect on when I started writing the first one in my dorm room during my freshman year of college. It amazes me how this story blossomed into what it is now. Kyrah's story is a beautiful rollercoaster that I absolutely love and appreciate. I'm proud of it. And I can't wait to write more stories that I can fall in love with.

As I emotionally write this letter, I want to say thank you to everyone who has given me a chance and followed this series. It can be tough being an indie author trying to get our stories out there. It can make us feel very vulnerable, especially those of us who do everything by ourselves including the editing. But in the end, I do this because I genuinely love it. So, I hope as you read through Kyrah's stories and the many stories to come, that you can feel all the hard work and love that I put into it.

To my babies, Kimberly and Ash, thank you for always being my tiny supporters who get so excited just seeing my books. I hope I am making you proud and am showing you that you can do anything you put your mind to.

To my amazing husband, DJ (Ashley)... the Anthony to my Kyrah... thank you so much for your continuous support and amazing love. You are my rock. You believed in me and this series when I didn't. You are my greatest blessing. Thank you for inspiring me and even helping me when I get crazy writer's block (lol). I hope I'm making you proud, too. And like you always tell me, "[I'm] gon' get us out the hood with these books".

Thank you for reading. Stick around for many more stories in the future.

P.S., your girl might be dipping a toe or two in spicy adult romances soon. (;

I love you.

God bless.

About Author

Karmen Scott, a wife, and mother of two, is an Augusta, Georgia native. She received her high school diploma from Lucy Craft Laney High School in 2014 and her bachelor's degree in marketing from Brenau University in 2020. She is currently working towards her master's in clinical mental health counseling from Walden University. However, Karmen's first love is writing.

Karmen attended Georgia Gwinnett College from 2014-2017 where she wrote her very first novel, Inexperienced her freshman year. Although she wears many hats, writing will always be her passion. She is the founder of Child of Purpose, LLC, and has a blog where she writes inspirational pieces to encourage her followers. Karmen hopes to continue her journey as a writer and published author in the years to come.

To learn more and follow her journey, visit www.childofpurpose blog.wordpress.com

INVITATION TO SALVATION

I know this is not usually something that is put at the
end of romance novels, but I am in a season where my
obedience is non-negotiable. And I will be honest and
say this is scary for me to do. But I have to do it.
With that, I want to say that if this is something that
doesn't interest you, I invite you to skim through or stop
here altogether. I promise you, I will not be offended.
However, I feel obligated to include this at the end of
my books, since all my written works are Christ-centered,
and the heart of my writing is to shine light on who he is
and how he has moved in my life through my characters.
I am not here to beat you over the head with the Bible
or try to force my beliefs on anybody. This is merely me
just doing what I feel God is telling me to do.
So, if you have read this far and wish to continue, keep
reading. If this is not for you, I thank you for being here
and reading my book. I appreciate you from the bottom
of my heart. And in case you haven't heard it today, I
love you!

CALL TO SALVATION

God's Word tells us in John 3:16 that He sent His one and only Son to die on the cross at Calvary for our sins. The entire world.

"For God so loved the world that He gave His only Begotten Son, that whosoever believes in him shall not perish, but have everlasting life."

Please know that despite everything that goes on in this world, God is still God and He loves you. And if that's something you can feel in your heart, please pray this prayer with me:

Heavenly Father, thank you for sending your Son to die for me. Please forgive me. I have made mistakes, but I believe that through your Son and because of his perfect Sacrifice, you have forgiven me for my sins. I confess that Jesus is Lord, and I believe He died on the cross just for me and rose again on the third day. I accept Jesus into my heart today and choose to follow you.

In Jesus' Name, Amen.

I love you so much. And I pray that God continues to bless you all the days of your life. May the Lord shine on you and be gracious to you. May the Lord show you His favor and give you His peace.